Junia

MICHAEL EDWARD GIESLER

JUNIA

Scepter

Published by Scepter Publishers, Inc.
www.scepterpublishers.org

ISBN 0–889334–64–2

FIRST PRINTING 2002
SECOND PRINTING 2003

Text composed in Adobe Caslon fonts

Printed in the United States of America

*To the early Christian martyrs
Agnes, Lucy, and Cecilia—
whose cheerfulness, courage, and unwavering faith
have provided the inspiration for this story.*

*Also to all those women and men
who would like to find Christ
in their ordinary lives.*

Contents

PRELUDE

I.

Discalus watched the crowds. It had been a slow morning; very few had stopped to buy his fish, freshly delivered from Ostia. He knew the reason though. There were some British captives recently brought from the isle to the north; they were supposed to be excellent spear throwers, and people were anxious to see them in the gladiatorial contest.

The storekeeper sat at his bench for a while. The noon sun was beating down hard. Later in the afternoon the ancient tenement house in the back would give some shade, he thought, but not now. An old woman walked up the road with a small boy at her side. She went up to the street lares* and cast a few bits of incense there. After mumbling some quick prayers, she moved on.

"Fishmonger!" a loud taunting voice suddenly resounded in his ears. How he hated that word! He looked up and saw a large Syrian man standing before him, with silver rings dangling from his ears. There was a strong perfumed scent about him. Discalus immediately recognized that he was from the household of Gladion, who had made himself a fortune in spices from India.

"Yes, sir," Discalus answered obsequiously.

"I don't have time to go to a better store, so I have to buy some of your . . . ," and at this the Syrian halted for a minute and put his fingers to his nose, ". . . some of your dainties."

Discalus felt a strong surge of anger. After all, he was a Roman citizen. His father had fought under Trajan, and

---

* A small stone shrine in honor of the protecting gods of the city. These shrines were very common in pagan times.

9

years ago he remembered his grandmother telling him that one of his family had served under the great Cincinnatus. How could he suffer such an insult from a Syrian upstart, who was not even a citizen?

"Give me five mackerels," the big man barked. Discalus obeyed; he knew better than to offend someone from a rich household. He could probably have the owner buy out his fish store in a moment; then he would have to go back to the farm. No, he would give the bully all he wanted, and smile about it as well.

"Don't you talk to my father that way," a small but resolute voice piped up from inside the shop. It was Discalus's eight-year-old son, Gaius. Discalus stepped out from his chair, walked to the back of the shop, and hit him on the mouth. "Be quiet!" he shouted. "Get back to your lessons."

When he returned he apologized profusely. "I'm sorry, sir, but my son has not yet learned to control his tongue." His customer laughed mockingly, "He probably has more courage than you'll ever have. Now give me my fish and let me be off."

Discalus gave him the fish, muttering the worst curses he could remember under his breath.

Shortly afterward, a ragged little fellow ran down the cobblestones in front of the shop. He looked about nine and was the son of Septimus the winekeeper. He was laughing, and had probably just played a prank on someone. A thin, wheezing dog trailed behind him. "Can Gaius play hoops?" he asked. The little fellow's brightness helped dispel some of Discalus's gloom. He felt a trace of remorse for having hit his son.

"Gaius," he said, "enough study. Go and play with your friend now." His small curly haired boy shuffled up from the back of the shop slowly. He was trying not to cry, but his father noted the tears. He looked away and waved his hand impatiently, "Go ahead now!" The boy slipped out quickly.

Discalus got up slowly, adjusted the shade over his table,

and walked down the street a bit. He was angry with himself; he shouldn't have struck his son like that. He was a brave lad for having defended him, and a good student too. His eyes fell upon a tiny plot of sand beneath the lares monument. There, clearly, he saw the outline of a fish, freshly traced. Discalus laughed to himself: it was the sign of the Christians, poor demented people who worshipped a criminal. He chuckled softly; it was comforting to know that there were some people worse off than himself.

II.

Not far away, Bombolinus was lucky enough to be close to the gladiatorial notices. The Thracian Scorpus would fight in four days in the great Flavian Amphitheatre. Bombo whistled through his teeth: Scorpus had been unbeaten in the last twenty matches. If he should lose, Bombo for one would cast thumbs up.*

He heard a man at his side say that there would also be a freedman in the arena who had been caught stealing a silver lampstead from his former owner. He would surely be fed to the lions. "I hope the poor wretch puts up more of a fight than the last robber," breathed a toothless old fellow next to him.

Bombolinus edged his way from the jostling crowd and, when clear, adjusted his soiled toga. He reached for a small wax tablet inside his toga and sauntered to the big wax bulletin boards, each of which had a separate announcement: the Emperor was sending a new legion to Britain; a fire had destroyed the tenement Fulvia located near Via Appia; new magistrates for city offices had been named.

Bombo's eyes lit up at this last notice; this is what he had been looking for. Elbowing his way closer to the bulletin board, he looked quickly through the list to see if any of his

---

* A sign given by Roman crowds signifying that they wished the gladiator's life be spared; thumbs down meant the opposite.

friends were named, even at the lowest levels. Nobody. Bombo cursed and turned away. He didn't even feel like reading the gossip boards this time. He was in no mood for that.

He walked slowly down Via Sacra, hoping to catch a glimpse of a wealthy friend or patron. How he yearned to have dinner at a fine house that evening! About fifty feet ahead he could see a litter* approaching, preceded by two dozen or so slaves: his heart leapt. Maybe it was Senator Gaius, his patron. No, it was a lady, a very made-up one. He recognized her immediately; it was Agrippina, widow of Calvus, who had been one of the wealthiest merchants in Rome. Now she was married to Antonius, the Praetor. But Bombo had heard that of late their money was dwindling; the gossip boards had carried a lot about her daughter, Livia. Bombo sighed loudly. How high and mighty Agrippina looked on the silver litter!

He would have to wait until tomorrow. Maybe he would meet someone at the baths. His friend Triclus was invited to dine just four days ago with a rich merchant, and all he did was to tell the old fellow a clever joke mixed with a little gossip from the forum.

It was almost sunset now. The poorer streets of Rome were already darkened by the long shadows cast by the five-story high tenements, but Bombo was in a merry mood. A glass of cheap posca wine would make him forget his cares; if he couldn't eat today at some senator's house, there would always be tomorrow, and if all else failed, Caesar's dole** would suffice.

III.

Bombo was up and out before dawn the next morning, but it was light enough for him to see the words that some bitter lover had scribbled on a wall: "*Ubi Verus, nihil verax*"

---

* From Latin *lectula*, an elaborate platform with a chair, carried by servants.
** Monthly rationing of grain for Rome's poorer classes.

("Where Verus is, there's nothing veracious"). He rushed along the street anxious to be the first at the door of Senator Gaius. Flavi, his wife, had cleaned his toga that night and even had given him a bit of perfume for his hair. This could be a big day for him. Perhaps the Senator would ask him to accompany him to the Senate . . . to applaud him. He knew that a big case was pending; an ex-governor of Bithynia was being tried for fraud and misuse of tax money. There was also an accusation that he had executed several provincials and one Roman citizen without proven cause.

Bombo had to fight the crowds on his way to the luxurious Esquiline hill, which was a fair distance from his tenement. Several slaves were already bounding toward the wealthier business district, probably to purchase fine wines and sweetmeats for their masters. Next to Discalus's fish stand, he could already hear Philippus's students declaiming.

Above all there was a rush of poor togaed Romans like himself, each skirting off to greet their patrons and to do the necessary favors for the day. "*Ave Triclus, Ave Julie,*" Bombo said in quick succession as his aspiring friends ran by. Everyone had anxious looks on their faces; today could be the day to meet a senator, or a rich merchant.

Bombolinus rushed on; he felt confident of his nimble wit now. And was he not well groomed today? He pushed away a homeless-looking dog that had moved in front of him and continued to run. But he had to stop at the corner of Via Sacra; a clattering of smart Praetorians* were marching down the broad street. Nobody dared to get in their way.

Bombo arrived just as the first orange streak graced the eastern sky, announcing the sun. From the top of the Esquiline he could see the entire sky. He reached the Senator's mansion with only two *clientes** ahead of him. "*Ave Syphe, Ave Timon,*" he said as he exchanged embraces with them, though he hated them both. He considered them rivals for

---

* Emperor's personal guards, attached to the Imperial Palace.
** Latin *clientes*, meaning political assistants.

the great man's attention, and he was determined to be the first to catch the Senator's ear that morning. Shortly afterward a whole crowd of *clientes* like himself arrived at the doorstep, but Bombo kept his first-place advantage. When the attendant opened the large iron gate, and the burly porter had inspected them all, he rushed through the atrium shouting, *"Ave Clarissime!"* (Hail great one!). He was the second to reach the noble Senator and the first to kiss his hand.

A SENATOR'S DAUGHTER

I.

Junia looked into the clear pool of her father's garden. It was bright enough to see her own reflection: the straight dark hair, which curled slightly on her forehead, the glistening blue eyes, the light olive complexion. She made a funny face and smiled at her image in the water. "Am I as pretty as Dido* was?" she asked herself, though she knew she was being vain.

Slowly she returned to the light green marble seat beneath the carefully trimmed poplar tree. She unraveled the scroll and read the lines again: "Dido was consumed with bitter tears, as Aeneas's ship sailed away." She closed her eyes and dreamed about the scene, as if she were poor Dido so disappointed in love, until she could almost feel tears coming to her eyes. But suddenly she felt embarrassed with it all. Inside her mind she could hear her father telling her, "Junia, Junia, never take foolishness seriously."

Still, it would feel sweet to cry.

Her dreamy mood was quickly interrupted by the arrival of her father's assistants. They began to rush in with their boisterous shouts of "*Ave, Ave,*" trying to get her father's attention in the atrium. She quickly went from feeling sweet to feeling irritated. "Why were they so loud? And they were dressed so poorly! Why, some of the household slaves had better manners, and they weren't even Romans," she thought to herself.

Junia rose slowly from the marble bench and walked to the arch near the entrance of the courtyard. In the corner

---

* Dido was the lover of Aeneas, who was the legendary ancestor of the Roman people. She was famed for her beauty.

stood a statue of Junius Brutus, who overthrew the last Roman king almost six hundred years before. Her father would often speak seriously of how the Republic needed men of his calibre today. She reached up and lightly flicked the ear of the somber looking statue. Father could be so naive at times! As if ten men, or a thousand men, like Brutus could break the power of a Caesar!

She stooped to pick up a shriveled leaf and threw it into the pool; the current from the triton's horn pushed it along aimlessly. The poet Virgil had compared dead souls to so many leaves swept by the wind into Hades. What would the philosophers say to that, she mused?

That gave her an idea. She clapped her hands quickly, and almost immediately her maidservant Cynthia appeared. She had been sitting behind the large red curtain, inside the courtyard, awaiting her mistress's command.

"Yes, Miss Junia."

"Go fetch my brother, Marcus," she said rather harshly, still feeling annoyed at the loud voices in the hall. "I would like to speak with him for a while."

"Begging your pardon, Miss, but Master Marcus left at dawn to hear a lecture of Strabo at the Juppiter Capitoline Temple."

"Theories again! Classes again!" the Roman girl replied wearily. "But come, you can do up my hair. I would like an ivory wreath and a little gold dust . . . not much. I've been invited to Marcia's house today. As soon as Father leaves for the Senate, we may go."

II.

After he had dismissed his *clientes*, Junia's father, Gaius Metellus Cimber, had his toga adjusted for his presentation in the Senate. The Curian purple stripe had to show just enough to indicate his authority without being ostentatious. His slave Syphon was nimble, and soon the complicated folds of the toga fell into perfect symmetry. Before leaving the mansion he gathered the necessary documents for his case, more than sufficient to convict Aulius, ex-governor of Bithynia.

Yet Gaius assumed nothing. According to the Stoa,* of which he considered himself a strict adherent, a man should do his duty and not expect to win—not even to be applauded. To defend a righteous cause for its own sake was reward enough for a virtuous man. But Gaius could not drive from his mind the thought of how good it would look for him to win.

His slaves and assistants were waiting at the door.

"All prepared, sir," reported Numo, one of his recently acquired slaves, and Gaius nodded to him. He liked Numo's tone: crisp, efficient, respectful. He was a good purchase.

Before leaving he waved to his daughter in the garden.

"Is your mother up yet?"

"I don't think so, Father," Junia answered with a sympathetic look.

She could tell that her father was upset by that, though he tried to show no reaction. It was one of his biggest cases, and Mother had not risen to wish him luck.

"Good luck, Father," Junia called to him encouragingly. "May the gods be with you . . . all of them!"

Gaius waved back to her. He stopped for a moment at the family lares altar next to the hearth and tossed a few pieces of incense on it. He was proud of his daughter and thanked the gods for her.

Eight slaves lowered a litter for him, and as soon as he had stepped in, they adjusted the shades for him. About thirty slaves and freedmen preceded him, about twenty-five in the rear. The procession started down the hill to Via Subura leading to the old forum** and to the Senate House. Gaius

---

* The Stoa was a Greek school of thought that stressed self-discipline and complete control of emotions. It became very popular among Romans, and its followers were called Stoics.

** The oldest of the Roman fora (or public squares); it was located between the Capitoline and Palatine hills.

could see the round curly head of Bombolinus. He was always the first to say "*Ave*," and a cheerful fellow. He thought to himself, "If he applauds me well in the Senate today, I'll invite him to dinner."

The slaves and freedmen pushed aside the teeming Roman populace; progress was fairly rapid. When they reached the old forum, Gaius's heart swelled with pride. The first large statue on the left was that of Scipio Africanus, victor over Hannibal in the battle of Zama more than three hundred years earlier. His family was related to Scipio's by blood; one of his distant relatives was Scipio's first in command, and later served as consul. The Senator looked at the statue with a certain melancholy. "No longer do we have Romans of your stamp, my brave Africanus," Junia's father thought to himself, "content to serve their country in battle, then return to civilian life. Now when a general wins a battle, he wants to be emperor."

Before reaching the Senate, he caught sight of the immense lustrous temple of Capitoline Jove. He knew his son, Marcus, was there, studying under Strabo the Athenian. A flash of anger crossed his breast; had he not asked Marcus to study oratory? That was far more practical in this day and age. Speculative philosophy was for the Greek, not for the practical Roman. He had hinted to Marcus that he would have liked to see him at his senate case. Not much chance of that, he thought to himself somewhat bitterly.

The case was held at the old Julian Senate House; about two-thirds of the senators were there, an excellent showing compared to other cases. It was rumored that Caesar had a personal interest in the trial.

Gaius did not have to be brilliant; the facts of the case spoke for themselves. Aulius had overtaxed the Bithynian provincials by three times; his personal accounts showed that. Furthermore, he had executed several of them on charges of subversion, with very little evidence. Nevertheless Gaius summoned up all his eloquence; he had studied his lines well, and knew when to grimace and when to throw up his hands deploringly. Some of his phrasing was from Cicero, though he was clever enough to introduce several of his own expressions as well. He even added satire to his presentation; did he not know the temptations of a governor, having been governor himself of Thrace for six years? Gaius prided himself on his unspotted record.

At key points, just where he wanted to hear them, Bombolinus would shout "*Euge, Euge*"* and clap his hands loudly. At the peak of the speech Bombo even hinted to a few dozing senators that now would be the best time to stand behind Gaius. Four of them did so.

Gaius won by an immense plurality, 280 to 40. Banishment was voted for the accused. It was Gaius's moment of triumph, perhaps the high point of his career, though he had his eyes on the consulship for next year. With this case, he could become a first-class friend of Caesar.

Several senators and other officials approached to congratulate him. "The voice of Cato himself!" shouted one. "Hortensius could not have spoken better!"** In the background one loud voice could be heard over them all: "He has made himself immortal today!" That brought many cheers. Gaius turned and saw that it was Bombolinus. "Friend, come to dinner tonight," the Senator called to him, and Bombo's heart leapt. He ran to kiss Gaius's hand, but several high-ranking senators brushed him aside.

As Gaius and his noble friends proceeded to the baths, Bombolinus ran home. He wanted to give his wife, Flavia, the news right away. Maybe now they could move down to the second floor of their tenement, where there was a living room with bright mosaics and a freshly painted fresco.

---

* Greek exclamation meaning "well done!"
** Cato and Hortensius were great political orators of the early Roman Republic, several hundred years before Gaius's time.

A DEAR FRIEND

I.

Shortly after her father left for the Senate, Junia set out in her light-blue litter, which was borne by eight sturdy Cappadocian slaves. She asked that the curtains be adjusted so that just enough sunlight would enter to allow her to read. The text she had was of Plato, the "divine Plato" as some called him. She liked the poetic style of his dialogues and wanted to speak to Marcus about them. The text was in Greek, which she could read fairly fluently; when she came across a word that she did not know, she would ask Cynthia, who sat beside her.

After a while she tired and opened the curtain a bit more. They were just about to ascend the Aventine and had passed most of the city crowds. Junia noticed a hastily scribbled drawing on a wall, which looked at first to be that of a man being crucified. But on closer inspection she saw that the body had the head of a donkey.

"What's that?" she asked with some disgust.

"That's a mockery of the Christians, Miss," her maidservant replied. "They apparently worship a crucified man who died about a hundred years ago. He was a Jewish criminal."

"The whole thing is such a sad delusion," Junia answered shaking her head. "My father says that most people in this cult are ignorant, uneducated types though. He thinks that the whole movement will disappear in fifty years or so."

"People say that they eat children in some of their ceremonies," Cynthia added with a certain glee.

Junia's eyes widened in disbelief, "You mean their own children?"

"I'm not sure," Cynthia admitted. "One of my friends from Dalmatia told me that she once heard some Christians talking about body and blood, and how a person had to eat these to be 'saved'—whatever that means. I still don't know whose body and blood she was talking about."

The litter came to a halt. "House of Diodorus Corinthus," bellowed one of the burly slave attendants who went before the litter clearing a way through the crowds. Junia stepped down gracefully, adjusting the folds of her robe in front of her. As she walked up the single step of Diodorus's mansion, Marcia ran out to her. The two girls embraced and kissed.

"It's been almost two weeks, Marcia. I've missed you."

"And I you, believe it or not," Marcia replied with a grin. Then she added, "Have you been reading those silly Greeks again?"

Junia laughed. It was so funny to hear Marcia say that . . . Marcia herself being Greek and her father being from Corinth. As soon as they entered the atrium, Marcia asked one of the household slaves to take Junia's cloak and put it in the great chamber.

Then she took her friend's hand and led her into the courtyard. Junia looked at the short, red-haired girl in front of her; she was always so much fun that it was hard to predict her next move. As soon as they reached the marble fountain in the courtyard, Marcia turned around and looked up at Junia, as if to tell a joke. Instead she put her hands on Junia's shoulders and began to jump off the ground. Junia could feel her breath blowing through her hair.

"Marcia, what are you doing?"

"Blowing the gold dust off your hair."

Junia found it very hard to get mad at her friend; what is more, she had suspected that Marcia would not approve of that fairly common ornamentation, extended among the wealthy classes. She always dressed very simply. The Roman girl defended herself with a little quip: "Now you've done it, you little Greek imp, all my Roman dignity blown away.

And why don't you do up your hair? Your father is one of the richest men in Rome, and you can surely hire a hairdresser."

She expected Marcia to keep jumping, but to her surprise she stopped suddenly and became quite serious. "Isn't this good enough?" she asked as she passed her hand through her short, curly hair, which was clean and quite attractive by itself.

"Good enough," Junia was forced to admit, as the two girls walked out to the garden.

Diodorus made a special effort to leave earlier that morning from the bank. He knew that Marcia was expecting her favorite friend and had promised that he would be home to meet her.

He found them both in the courtyard. Marcia ran up to him quickly and gave him a warm embrace. "Papa! We're being intellectuals today. We've been translating ·Virgil's *Aeneid* into Greek. A great exercise! Junia's pretty good, you know . . . for a Roman." And at that she turned to Junia, and winked mischievously.

Junia smiled sedately and walked up to Marcia's father. Though she was always polite to Diodorus, she never particularly liked him. Apart from his appearance (he was short and prematurely bald), she considered him exaggerated in his manner at times, and a rather careless dresser. For her aristocratic tastes, he also seemed too much concerned about money, though he had worked long and hard to obtain his present position and was considered by all to be scrupulously honest. As she approached, Diodorus bowed deeply and kissed her hand.

"Your father has had a magnificent triumph in the Senate today, dear Mistress Junia. All of Rome is talking about it. I am honored to have his daughter in my house."

Junia thanked him politely, but could not hide a certain coldness in her voice. Though she didn't want it, her words seemed to come out that way.

Diodorus sensed her reserved reply, but immediately smiled and kept up the conversation. "You must be tired from your trip here. Why don't we have something to eat?"

Diodorus's house attendants had set the most elegant table in the dining area. When she entered the room, Junia's eyes lit up. The servants were beautifully attired, and the sweetmeats and wine were placed artistically on the marble table. There was a vase of flowers in front of the main mosaic and a very pleasant scent in the air.

"Syrian incense," Marcia whispered to her. "I thought you'd like it."

But the biggest surprise was yet to be seen. In the center of the main table a silver platter had been placed, with a cover. A little piece of papyrus was attached to it with the inscription: "*Juniae, ut valeas semper*" (For Junia: may you always be well). The Roman girl lifted the cover slowly and smiled appreciatively.

"Cyprian dates. My favorite dish. Marcia, how did you get them?"

"I didn't," her friend answered. "My father did."

The daughter of Gaius looked down for a moment. She felt ashamed for her coldness to Diodorus a few minutes earlier. But when she turned to thank him, he had gone.

"Master Diodorus has gone to the central bank," the doorman announced.

Junia inwardly resolved to thank him the next time they met . . . not realizing that this would be the last time she would ever see him.

II.

Junia arrived home very happy that day; being with Marcia always made her more cheerful. She especially enjoyed Marcia's sense of humor, always witty, always cosmopolitan. If she weren't so short and stocky, Junia often reflected, she could easily have a high-born Roman for a suitor.

Junia's mother, Aurelia, was in her chamber when her young daughter arrived. She was having her hair lifted, then curled, with an Armenian headset that Gaius had bought for her a month prior. She was not like many Roman ladies who fussed over every wave and curl and who would order maidservants beaten for small errors. But she did take the operation very seriously, as if it were some kind of drama and she was the heroine.

Aurelia did not notice her daughter enter, and Junia, with Marcia's fun still inspiring her, motioned the hairdresser away. She took the slave's position and quietly worked at a rather stubborn lock of hair that would not fold behind the headset. Not being as skilled as the slave, though, she could not weave it in properly. Before her mother could discover who it was, however, Junia thought she would imitate her friend. She stood up quietly and suddenly shouted "Mama!" at the same time blowing through her hair.

Aurelia shrieked loudly and bolted upright as if lightning had struck her. When she turned and saw her smiling daughter, she looked crossly for a moment and then broke into a rather silly grin.

"Where have you been this morning, daughter of Gaius?" she said, trying to regain her composure.

"Don't you remember, Mother? I told you yesterday. At Marcia's home."

"Oh, yes," her mother said absently, as she posed once again for the hairdresser to work. "That little Greek girl."

"Not so little, Mama," Junia's voice grew suddenly serious. "In some ways I think she's much bigger than I am."

"Nonsense, my child! You're taller and much more beautiful than she is . . . my own sweet Junia," she added as she gave her an affectionate pat on the hand. "By the way, today I go to the Mithran play with Agrippina."

Junia felt annoyed with her mother. She hadn't even spoken about Gaius's case that day.

"Did you hear about Father's victory today in the Senate?"

Aurelia was looking intensely once again at her hair in the mirror. "Oh, yes," she said absently, "that . . . he did well, I suppose."

"Yes, Mother, as usual," Junia droned back to her, in a purposely dull tone of voice. It bothered her that she was so passive about things and suddenly felt quite angry with her.

At that moment one of the attending slaves entered the chamber. "Master Marcus has arrived," he announced with a rather thick Hispanic accent.

III.

Junia met her brother, Marcus, in the atrium. He was wearing a simple tunic* and was breathing heavily, as if he had just run into the house.

"Shame on you, Marcus, going to the street without your toga! What would Father say?" Junia knew that her brother hated to wear a toga, since he considered himself to be a citizen of the world, not just of Rome.

"And walking through the streets like a plebeian! You're perspiring like an ordinary street laborer . . ."; this she added with some irritation. It was obvious that he didn't want to live like an aristocrat and she resented that.

Marcus brushed aside her comments; he was used to his sister's teasing ways.

"Strabo was far more heated than I am right now," he said. "You should have heard him speak today."

"Why? Is there another theory in the air?"

"Fairly new," he replied, "as philosophies go. It's about a hundred years old. But it has been underground until now, at least in intellectual circles."

Brother and sister walked through the atrium into the courtyard. It was about two o'clock, and the sun was near its zenith. They sat in the shade of a leafy cypress, after Marcus

---

* Full-length garment reaching to ankles, worn by both men and women.

had refreshed himself in the clear reflecting pool that Junia sometimes used as a mirror. He set down the three voluminous scrolls that he had carried with him from Strabo's academy near the Juppiter temple.

'You know how Strabo has been trying for the last year to find a solution, or synthesis, for Stoic and Platonist ideals. He wanted to connect the high moral standards and serenity of the Stoics with the contemplation and enthusiasm of the Platonists. It was a problem that bothered me also, and we had discussed it many times."

"Yes, I remember," added Junia. "Not only you and Strabo, but you and I."

"Exactly. Well about one month ago, Strabo and I thought we had found the answer in Gnosis."

"*Gnosis*? The Greek word for knowledge?"

"Yes, it's a system of secret knowledge that is supposed to make one perfectly happy, though it is very difficult to attain. Strabo spoke with several of these Gnostics, and they convinced him to try their system. He and I have been learning their complicated formulas. They have a supra-world of eons which somewhat parallels Plato's world of ideas."

"Is that the theory that you spoke about at first?"

"No," Marcus answered with excitement. Junia smiled patronizingly; she especially enjoyed her brother when he became excited about some intellectual theme.

"You see, Junia, Strabo has met someone who has a completely different theory and is totally against the Gnostics. He speaks of an eternal happiness that comes from self-sacrifice."

"Self-sacrifice?" his sister asked. "That sounds perfectly awful. Why would anybody want to do such a thing?"

"I don't really know much more. Strabo was very excited about it this morning. Oh, yes! He also said that this new philosophy has something to do with a Logos or Word, but not in the same sense that the Gnostics or old Heraclitus used it."

"It does sound interesting," Junia conceded. "Who is this new philosopher?"

"His name is Justin, and he's originally from Palestine, though he has travelled all over the world. Very articulate man, according to Strabo. But I haven't told you the biggest news of all."

"What's that?"

"This Justin is supposed to be a Christian, or at least associated with them."

"What?" exclaimed his sister. "I thought these Christians were too ignorant to have a philosopher of their own; this is quite a development."

"No doubt," Marcus replied quickly. "But a good idea is a good idea, no matter from where it comes. I intend to pursue the matter."

Junia stiffened suddenly. "Marcus," she whispered to him intensely, almost harshly, "don't be silly. This man is a *Christian*. Don't get involved with a group of superstitious criminals. That's what they are, you know."

The son of Gaius, four years older than his sister, looked at her mysteriously. He stroked his light brown beard gently and took up his scrolls. "We'll see," he said, and walked into his chamber.

IV.

The next morning Aurelia called her daughter to her room. Junia found her still in bed, though the servants were bringing her some breakfast, as was her custom.

"Junia, I would like you to pay a visit today."

The Roman girl sat alongside the large bed and gently rubbed her mother's knees. She felt sorry for having made fun of her yesterday. She also knew that Aurelia very rarely asked her to do anything unless her father was in some way behind it.

"With whom, Mother?"

"With Livia, daughter of Antonius."

Junia bolted upright and shook her head vigorously. "With Livia! You know I can't stand her; she thinks she's the most attractive girl in Rome, and it's all makeup. No, I don't want to go."

Aurelia took her by the hand.

"Your father wants it so. Livia's stepfather, Antonius, has just been named Praetor,* and it would be good if some members of our family socialized with them more. Besides, Junia," and at this her eyes lit up like a girl of twelve, "just think: you'll have a chance to see some of the new Greek plays and a chariot race."

Junia resigned herself. She didn't much care for the Greek mimes or the races, but she had a strong sense of duty toward her father, whom she had always tried to obey. What is more . . . and here a reassuring smile crossed her lips . . . she could invite Marcia. Marcia's good humor would help take away some of Livia's sting.

After leaving her mother's room, Junia sent a special messenger to Marcia's house, with instructions to return immediately. He was to ask if Marcia could go to the games with her, and she included a personal note to her friend to make it more important.

The messenger returned as Junia was reading a speech for the Senate that her father had given her.

"What's her response?" Junia asked him with some anxiety in her voice.

"Mistress Marcia is very sorry, but she cannot go to the games today."

Junia stamped her foot on the floor and shook her head, which was a habit of hers when she was angry.

"Did she give any reason?"

"No, Miss Junia, she simply said that it was not possible for her to go today but that she hopes to see you tomorrow."

* One of the highest magistrative offices in Rome.

Her face reddened suddenly.

"Well, we'll see about that. I just may not feel like seeing her tomorrow."

V.

On a green field far from Rome, a young Roman centurion named Quintus was preparing his squadron for battle. Their opponents, the Parthians, were formidable, particularly their archers and cavalry. It was a shame, Quintus thought, that most of the Roman cavalrymen and archers had been detached to Macedonia just two weeks earlier. This would be a very rough battle.

As the Roman line advanced, the enemy archers seemed to be playing with them: a few arrows here, a few arrows there. No casualties. But as the distance between them became shorter, the shower of arrows increased. Men began to curse as the pointed steel grazed their helmets; two rows ahead, one soldier had already fallen, pierced through the eye.

Quintus felt frustrated; his men were used to a strong hand-to-hand combat. This wasn't war; it was dodging, he thought. Still the shield was proving to be the best defense. Suddenly someone shouted "Cavalry to the right!" and Quintus could hear loud cries and thuds to the right of the cohort.* Obeying his orders, the centurion ordered his soldiers not to turn but to keep marching on against the archers.

Very shortly, however, the cries to the right grew louder, and the thudding of hoofs grew closer. Quintus turned, and to his horror he could see over one hundred Parthian cavalrymen chopping down his men. The soldiers fought bravely but did not have enough room to use their javelins. Since there was no higher officer available, Quintus had to make a quick decision.

* A tenth of a legion, or approximately 600 men.

"Extend the lines," he shouted, and his men quickly disengaged from their tight formation and formed a long line. The arrows came more heavily, and three of his men fell. He rushed to the first line and shouted, "At the horses!" Ninety-five javelins found their mark. Those horses not killed or wounded were spooked by the sudden move and began running back, bumping into each other. About thirty enemy cavalrymen fell to the ground, where the legionaries made quick work of them with their broadswords. The division behind Quintus followed suit, extending its lines and directing its javelins at the cavalrymen. When they saw the cavalry routed, the archers quickly retreated.

A great shout of triumph followed. Hundreds of Roman soldiers were shouting "Hail Quintus" as word spread of his courage and level-headedness.

Quintus felt his heart swell with the shouts. His second-in-command embraced him, and the soldiers of his cohort were thronging around him. As they lifted him on their shoulders, he thought of his father, Cassianus, one of Hadrian's greatest generals, who had died about a year before in Egypt. How proud he would have been! And wouldn't this mean that now he had a chance for the Praetorian Guard in Rome? He might even be given the command of a garrison, or be made assistant to the Prefect himself.

His thoughts raced on as the triumphant troops reached headquarters. Quite unexpectedly, though, his exultant mood was dampened. In the distance Quintus could see three crosses with bodies hanging from them, in a field just to the north of the barricaded fort. He felt a vague feeling of irritation, as if their dismal presence took away his glory at that moment.

"Must be Christians," he muttered to himself. He looked away and quickly forgot the grim spectacle.

"Hail Quintus!" another shout arose.

VI.

Livia and Junia were the two most eligible young women in Rome at that time, but Livia, spurred by her mother, felt almost a compulsive need to compete. She hoped to show everyone on the day of the races that while she could not outdo Junia in beauty or education, she could at least attract more attention.

One way was through gossip. From the first moment, when Livia with a large group of her friends met Junia at the Circus Maximus, she began to repeat the latest rumors and innuendos that she had heard.

"They say that Vulpina is about to elope with Decimus, that fledgling senator from Gaul. Apparently her husband doesn't care; he's too busy making money. What's more, I've seen him twice with Portia at the gladiatorial games. The next thing you know, they'll be going to the baths together!"

Livia's comment brought loud laughter from the four young men and two women who sat with them at the Circus. Most were rather high-born playboys from wealthy families in the city, though one was a simple opportunist, who had eagerly latched on to Livia and her friends. Livia soon let Junia know that they were all her suitors.

The pantomimes before the chariot race were performed by a group of Corinthian players. Most of the acts were gross adaptations from more serious Greek plays; the constant reference to sexual perversion and strange love affairs brought loud guffaws from the crowd. At one point Livia turned to Junia and whispered, "By the way, is your brother still visiting that Cybele priestess?"

Junia's eyes flashed with resentment. That was something that had deeply hurt her family, especially her father. Though it had occurred almost two years before, Gaius's enemies would still bring it up.

"Livia," Junia said in a low but firm voice, "that's over.

And Marcus realized that it was a big mistake. Have the nobility, if you can muster it, to keep quiet about it."

The other young woman smiled. "But I am, my dear. I'm whispering it, you know."

After the chariot races, the entire group went to Livia's mansion for a banquet. Junia was given all the external honors proper to a senator's daughter; she travelled in a separate litter borne by eight slaves and lead by twenty more. She was met at the door by the newly elected quaestor and his wife, Agrippina, and escorted to a specially prepared guest chamber where she could rest and prepare for the banquet. Two Numidian maids attended to her more personal needs.

But Junia wasn't happy. She noted a definite coldness in Agrippina's welcome. Livia's attitude had galled her from the start, but she did not want to fight her back on the same terms. With all the impetuousness of her youth she wanted to do something wild that would shock Livia and her whole entourage, but at the same time she realized her social position and her duty to her father.

The dinner was lavish, and the wine flowed freely. Though the food was costly, and much of it imported, the daughter of Gaius ate little; she would have preferred a more simple meal with Marcia. She smiled to herself as she thought of the Greek girl's charm and cleverness and kept looking toward the door to see if she might come after all.

"Junia dearest," it was the voice of Agrippina. "I would like to introduce you to Rodon, a student of philosophy from Athens. Perhaps you would like to speak with him; I know that you and your brother are interested in that sort of thing."

Junia looked up at Livia's mother and nodded gratefully. She seemed sincere for this once. It was kind of her to note that she was tired of all the coarse jokes, and would like to meet someone different.

Rodon was a tall young man with a black beard and sparkling dark eyes. His talk was witty, filled with philosophical and literary allusions. Like all Greeks he was very well informed about politics in the city, and Junia found his Athenian accent charming.

"Your father did very well yesterday, didn't he?"

Junia liked that. It was probably the best thing that any young man could have said to her, to win her favor. But she tried to play down her own emotion.

"That's what everybody is saying," she answered in a matter-of-fact tone of voice. "I thank you for the compliment, on his behalf."

"Yes, he did well," Rodon continued as if he had not heard her, "although he made two mistakes."

Junia acted offended, though inwardly she was curious. She had always liked men who spoke their minds, especially if they could do so with a certain authority.

"What do you mean?" she replied in a hurt tone of voice. "He won the case, didn't he? And there was an ovation when he finished. And afterward . . ."

"Yes, I know all that," Rodon interrupted. "But he moved his hands too much, and his voice was strained at times. Also he mumbled two of his lines."

"If that's true, I must admit that you're quite observant," Junia answered, trying to remain nonchalant. "Where did you study by the way?"

As the conversation continued, Rodon asked if she wanted more wine. At first she declined, but Rodon spoke so well, and appeared to her so cleverly frank about everything he said, that she began to drink more wine with him. Little by little she found herself giggling at every comment that he made.

The other diners had also drunk a great deal, and some of the men began to lean closer to their lady companions, whispering things that made many of them smile knowingly. Livia's father, Antonius, felt it was the right moment to bring in the Dionysian dancers, with their exotic mixture of religion and promiscuity. They began to beat their drums and sing seductive songs, both in Greek and Latin.

It was at that point that Rodon moved closer to his attractive companion. "You're fair as a moonbeam, dearest Junia. Let's take a stroll in the garden. See how the stars are inviting us," he whispered as he put his arm around her.

Junia could feel, rising within her, a strong surge of passion. Her head was spinning with the wine that Rodon had given her, and her heart was pounding with the drums of the Dionysian priests and priestesses. It would have been very easy to accept the young man's invitation; she knew what he wanted to do. Livia and her companions already had left the banquet room.

Self-control. Discipline. They were words and ideals that her father had taught her from early childhood. He had always taught her that real virtue was proven in difficult situations. She forced herself to remember. Though she felt quite attracted to Rodon at that moment, she could not forget that she was the daughter of Gaius.

Slowly, almost majestically, she rose to her feet. She did not even look at him. "I feel ill," she said to Agrippina, who was standing close by and seemed to be observing closely everything she was doing. "Please take me to the guest chamber and call for my litter."

VII.

The next morning Junia felt quite ill; this time it wasn't feigned. She couldn't tell if it was something she had eaten or drunk at Livia's, or if it had been a cold draft. At any rate she was coughing hard, and her forehead was moist and feverish. She had not been able to sleep that night.

Gaius had a doctor come that same morning. He prescribed cold compresses for the forehead and a certain potion which he claimed was very effective for eliminating congestion, and which he had received from a Thracian physician years before. It was foul tasting, but Junia took it obediently.

It seemed to help little, however, and Junia's illness went on for several days. She saw little of her family, and was mostly attended by the slaves. Her father was very busy at the time, since the Senate was about to adjourn for the summer, and several pending matters had to be resolved. Aurelia was convinced that her daughter had some form of the plague and would not enter her chamber. Marcus was very taken with his studies; once in a while he would drop in for a short time to exchange some intellectual comment, but he would not detain himself. Since Junia had a headache, she was not the best conversationalist. And what Marcus liked most was the flow of new ideas.

Finally, after insisting, Junia managed to see her father before he retired for the night. She was anxious to tell him about the banquet and how she had acted; she was convinced that he would be very proud of her. What is more, she wanted him to hold her hand, or at least visit for a while, and tell her that she would be well soon.

The senator, quite tired from his day's work, came into the room and looked at his daughter for a while, without saying a word. His face was stern. Finally, in a grave tone of voice, he said, "Junia, this is a caprice."

"No, Father, it's not that way!" his daughter protested. "I have so much to tell you. Do you remember that banquet at Livia's that you wanted me . . ."

"Noble souls suffer in silence," her father interrupted her. "You seem to let this illness control your emotions too much, Junia. You will overcome this illness; convince yourself that you want to. That is all that matters."

"Yes, Father. I know," Junia replied as she lowered her glance to her legs. She could feel tears forming in her eyes and was ashamed of her weakness. Then she looked up slowly and asked almost timidly, "Could you stay with me, Father, like when I was little?" She remembered how he would take her upon his lap and tell her bedtime stories. She felt that she needed his attention now, more than anything else.

"Junia," her father answered her in a firm voice, "you must let reason be your guide. A longer visit would not be prudent; there is danger of contagion. I'll have some books brought to you tomorrow, and perhaps a flautist from the Orient who can play for you. That will soothe you a bit."

His daughter looked away from him. "Very well, Father," she said in a barely audible voice.

"Good night, then, Daughter," the Senator replied, as he quietly left the room. He was satisfied with the lesson that he had given her. Nevertheless, as he walked away, he thought that he heard a muffled sob coming from the room. "How weak is woman," he thought to himself.

VIII.

The next morning Junia felt more poorly than any other day. Though her fever and headache continued as before, she felt like running away. She could not forgive her father for his attitude. She knew that he was right but that did not satisfy her. In the back of her mind she was beginning to think that she should have said yes to that amorous Greek at Livia's party. "After all, almost everyone my age in Rome is having some kind of affair," she thought. "Why should I be the only virtuous one?"

At that moment Cynthia stepped into the room, with a contented smile on her face. "Miss Junia, Miss Marcia is here to see you."

Junia's heart skipped for a moment. She was overjoyed to hear that Marcia had come. But she also remembered that Marcia had not wanted to go with her that day to the games and the banquet. If Marcia had been there, as a matter of fact, she may not have become ill. Her first reaction of joy turned to resentment, as she told Cynthia harshly: "Tell her that it's my turn to refuse an invitation. I don't want to see her."

Cynthia tried to get her mistress to reconsider a bit; she too found Marcia delightful. But her mistress remained adamant, and she left the room as commanded. Junia felt a pang of regret as she left and was about to change her mind, but her pride checked her. She didn't need Marcia to overcome this, she kept telling herself.

Shortly afterward she heard excited whispering and laughing outside of the door. "What's going on out there?" Junia asked irritably.

"Oh, we're just discussing you, and how you're such a *nobli-nubli*.* You see, I'm bribing Cynthia to let me in."

"Marcia!" the Roman girl exclaimed without thinking as soon as she recognized her friend's voice. It was hard for her to remain irritated any longer. She really couldn't hide her delight and began to chuckle to herself.

"May I come in?" Marcia asked, this time more softly.

Junia remembered that she was supposed to be angry.

"Alright," she replied, "but only for a few moments."

Marcia walked up to her bedside. She was smiling broadly, which seemed to light up her red hair and freckles even more.

"How I've missed you, Junia!" she exclaimed as she kissed her friend on the forehead. "You're prettier than ever, even when you're sick. How I envy you!"

"Marcia," Junia cried out. "You'll catch my sickness. Be careful! You're crazy!" But right after she said it, she couldn't help smiling gratefully for her friend's affection.

"Oh, that's alright," Marcia responded cheerfully while taking the patient's hand in hers. "You see, I'm basically immune; it's part of being from Corinth.** Contagious diseases have never really agreed with me."

At that Junia laughed out loud, for the first time in several days. She took Marcia's hand and held it for a while.

"You did play a bad trick on me, you know."

---

* A play on words in Latin referring to Junia, meaning noble (*nobilis*) and marriageable at the same time (*nubilis*).

** Corinth was one of the crossroads cities of the Roman Empire, filled with many different kinds of people—and therefore diseases.

"When was that, Junia?"

"When you didn't accept my invitation and go to the banquet at Livia's. I had an awful time."

Marcia stopped smiling for a minute. She placed her other hand on top of Junia's and stroked it gently. "Dear Junia, please try to understand. That's precisely why I could not go with you; I knew that you would have a terrible time . . . and me too. But there was nothing I could do, because I knew that you had to go. I'm so sorry."

Her sick friend smiled faintly at first, then more broadly, as Marcia's words and their real meaning slowly penetrated her mind. She realized that she had judged her friend too quickly, and felt much more at ease.

"What do you have beside you, Marcia?"

"A poem."

"A poem? By whom?"

"By me."

"By you? Not a very noted author, I must say," Junia replied teasingly.

"Not noted perhaps," Marcia responded good naturedly, "but very promising."

"We'll be the judges of that, dear girl. And to whom is it dedicated?"

"To you."

"To me? Not very noted either."

And at that all three girls broke into laughter. Junia was the first to speak after they had calmed down a bit.

"Come now, read it, Marcia. Cynthia and I will listen to it carefully, and afterward we will give you our critique."

At that point Marcia stood up and passed her hand through her curly red hair in a dignified fashion, pretending to be a famous poet. Cynthia and her mistress could not help laughing, to which Marcia responded with a kind of mock indignation. In the end she read her poem, in Latin, but mixed with many Greek words. It was a humorous piece about how people catch colds and the best way to get rid of a sneeze.

After Marcia's visit, Junia's convalescence sped along. The Greek girl visited her every day; they read together, played table games, and above all, laughed a lot. One day, when Junia could eat normally, Marcia brought her a surprise. "Today you have something special, pretty one," Marcia kidded her as soon as she entered the room. She quickly showed her friend a handsomely wrapped package. Junia opened it eagerly, and to her delight, she saw a perfectly arranged row of Cyprian dates.

The Roman girl looked up at her friend. Suddenly, as if for the first time, she was aware of all the kindness that Marcia had brought to her during the past weeks. She felt a strong feeling of gratitude to her, but she was embarrassed that her friend should notice it.

"You're very good to me, Marcia. I don't know how to repay you."

"No," interjected Marcia. "Don't thank *me*. They're from my father; he remembered that you liked them."

Junia smiled gently and bit her lip.

"Tell your father," she said, "that I am very thankful, and also that I'm sorry for my rudeness to him in the past."

IX.

Shortly after Junia's recovery, Gaius Metellus began to make plans to transfer his family to his country villa in Latium, as he did every July and August. He insisted on a certain austerity in the preparation and made sure that the women, especially his wife, would take only the necessary. "We have plenty of excellent fineries in the villa," he reminded them.

As a way to assure speed and accuracy, the Senator asked his daughter to coordinate the packing. He trusted Junia's good sense and gave her careful instructions on weight and space limitations. He told her frankly, "Your brother is too wrapped up in his philosophy, I'm afraid; and your mother, with putting on her makeup. That leaves you."

Junia made an inventory of all that she thought the family would need that summer and showed it to her father. "Good," he said. "You're a smart girl. But I notice that you're bringing very little for yourself. I think you could take more cosmetics with you."

Junia smiled back at him whimsically.

"Oh, Father, how unstoical of you! I don't need so many cosmetics, you know." And then she added more seriously, "Marcia has taught me that."

Before her family left, Junia paid a final visit to her friend. After greeting each other, they sat down to speak in the courtyard. For some reason Marcia appeared very serious, almost somber, which of course was completely unlike her.

"Marcia," Junia teased her gently, "why do you look so solemn today?"

Her friend answered her slowly. "I guess there are two reasons. The first is because you're leaving Rome, and I shall miss you dearly. That's reason enough. And the second . . .

At this point she halted her speech and looked to the ground.

"Yes, Marcia, and the second reason?"

"It's so hard to explain, Junia. I can't do it. It will take a long time. I've been wanting to tell you something very important, but it will take me a long time."

Junia had never heard her friend speak that way before. She suddenly had an idea, which she had been considering before, that would enable her to spend more time with Marcia. Now seemed to be the perfect opportunity to ask her about it.

"Marcia," Junia was smiling warmly at her friend, "I have a good solution. Why don't you come to our country villa for a time this summer? We would have much more time to talk then."

Marcia responded immediately and with her usual enthusiasm.

"That's a wonderful idea! And I am sure that Father

wouldn't mind, since he respects you and your family so much. And then . . . "—her voice lowered a bit, as if holding something back—"and then I can tell you."

"Then you can tell me? Marcia, it all sounds so mysterious," Junia answered lightheartedly.

"Yes, it is a mystery, and it's so wonderful at the same time. It means everything to me." Marcia's dark eyes brightened as she spoke, and her voice seemed more confident.

"It means everything to you? That makes me a little jealous. Come on, tell me now."

"I can't. I should wait a bit longer, and think."

"Very well," her friend responded resolutely. "In two weeks we'll be waiting for you in the villa. That should give me time to get established and to put things in order."

The two girls embraced each other excitedly and said goodbye.

X.

It was as Quintus had suspected. His bravery had not gone unnoticed. Within a month, he received word that he had been promoted; but not for two months did he learn his exact position. When he heard it at last, he was amazed. He had been appointed Assistant Prefect of the Praetorian Guard in Rome . . . the Emperor's personal guard.

The young Roman reflected about it. Surely it was not just for the battle, but because his father had been a close friend of Hadrian and one of his best commanders. Quintus was noble enough to feel a bit displeased about his sudden rise to power. He would have preferred to remain in the field for a while longer, and to have earned his promotion with greater merits. But he was not unhappy about his prospects and of course accepted the appointment gladly.

His first march through the streets of Rome was well heralded. He marched proudly, and began to swagger a bit like the other Praetorians. At first he felt that it was breach of military discipline, but the force of custom and the other Praetorians' attitude took their effect on him. He even began to feel a certain disdain for the commoners on the street, though he tried to check that reaction.

Once in a while Quintus would go carousing with the other soldiers, but he was never able to banish the feeling of repugnance inside of him. The women, the experience, seemed cheap to him. He was never satisfied with the drinking bouts either, at which some of his fellow guards excelled; he held back frequently and returned to the barracks. Toward the middle of July, he received a letter from one of the government offices on the Caelian hill:

THE EMPEROR DIRECTS YOU TO DELIVER, BY WORD OF MOUTH, THE FOLLOWING MESSAGE TO GAIUS METELLUS CIMBER, IN HIS VILLA IN LATIUM; THAT THE EMPEROR IS PLEASED WITH HIS PROSECUTION OF AULIUS, AND THAT HE HEREBY INVITES THE SENATOR TO PRESENT HIMSELF AS A CANDIDATE FOR CONSUL IN THE FALL. THE EMPEROR ALSO ENJOINS YOUR TOTAL DISCRETION IN THIS MATTER.

Quintus whistled to himself as he read it. The consulship was the highest political office that a man could hold in Rome. He had heard of Gaius before and also had heard that his daughter was one of the most beautiful and intelligent young women in Rome. He was pleased that the Emperor had entrusted a confidential matter to him and made plans for the journey immediately.

Quintus found the Senator's family established in their villa and delivered the message quickly. The Senator gathered his household together, including his most trusted slaves, and let them know the joyful news. He also ordered a special dinner that day, with freshly hunted pheasants and the best wines available.

Assistant Prefect Quintus did not hide his appreciation when the Senator invited him to be the guest of honor. Nor could he hide his admiration for Junia. In all his travels he had not seen a girl so beautifully endowed, both in mind and body. When not speaking with the Senator, he looked at his daughter and at one point, found himself staring at her. Junia caught his glance and smiled back shyly. Quintus felt embarrassed and quickly looked away, but he could feel his heart pounding strongly.

"Prefect Quintus, could you tell us about your campaigns in Dacia?" the Senator began after the main course had been served.

Quintus was glad for the opportunity. Speaking about military campaigns with his Praetorian companions was far more difficult; they would make gruff comparisons between him and others with more experience in the field. And there was always a wagging tongue that would remind him that after all he was Cassianus's son and that he had gotten his appointment through connections. Here, in this pleasant family atmosphere, he felt more free and could perhaps exaggerate a bit.

"I was in Dacia, in charge of a cohort for two years, fighting against the Parthians." And Quintus began to narrate the various battles that he had seen and waged, finishing with the battle that had made him famous. He tried to remain objective as he spoke, but he found himself raising the number of archers and enemy cavalrymen. Quintus became more and more heated as he continued his story, and in the end he exclaimed, "Yes, and that's how we won that battle, thanks not only to me but to the obedience and discipline of the Roman Army."

Marcus had listened patiently up to that point, though he had felt annoyed at Quintus's manner of glorifying his achievements. He did not agree that the Roman army had made Rome great and would contain himself no longer.

"Just a minute, Quintus," Marcus tried to speak steadily, but could not hide a tone of irritation in his voice. "You soldiers always seem to be saying that you make Rome great. What if I told you that the philosophers make Rome great?"

Quintus was not sure how to react to Marcus. Had he been in the barracks, his very question would have brought howls of laughter and, quite possibly, a punch in the face. But here in this more refined atmosphere he chose to spar with Marcus on his own ground.

"Philosophers have many ideas, it seems to me, and complex words. They bring up interesting topics for conversation, but quite frankly, they don't build empires."

"I agree that words don't build empires but neither does the force of arms. Weapons and soldiers can impose authority for a while, but ideas last longer and have greater influence."

Quintus shook his head. He felt that not only he but his fellow soldiers were being insulted. With some annoyance he answered, "I really can't understand you bookish fellows. You do nothing but read and discuss theories all day. How can you possibly hope to keep Rome strong and defend her from her enemies?"

Marcus's eyes flashed with anger. "And how can you soldiers of the Praetorian Guard hope to defend Rome when all you do is drink and . . ."

"Marcus, please. Control your tongue," Aurelia intervened, with a certain stately calm in her voice. "Remember that Quintus is our guest and has brought us very welcome news. You must tell him that you're sorry."

There was an awkward silence. Marcus made as if to speak, but could not. Quintus began to shift on his dinner couch uneasily. Senator Gaius was also at a loss. He didn't want to offend his guest, but he was also hurt that neither of the two had mentioned the role of the Senate in making Rome great.

At that point a cheerful feminine voice broke the impasse. It was Junia, who had been following the conversation carefully, but without saying a word.

"Let me suggest that none of you are right. It was neither the army, nor philosophers, nor the Senate . . . begging your pardon, Father," she added as she winked at him because she knew what he was thinking. "It was something that you have all forgotten. I'll show you what has made Rome great."

She left the room and returned with a bronze lyre* in her hands. "Let me sing you all a little song that a friend taught me," she said, with a clever smile on her lips.

The entire group was relieved for the pleasant and timely change of topic and listened gratefully to Junia as she sang a little tune that her Corinthian friend had taught her:

> *I heard it once said*
> *and know it to be true*
> *so now I gently repeat it to you*
> *that music soothes, both now and then*
> *what savage beats in the hearts of men.*

The melody, and the timely words, brought claps of approval from everybody. At their request she played more tunes, sometimes singing in Greek, sometimes in Latin. Cynthia accompanied her in one of the longer songs.

"Dear sister," Marcus exclaimed at the end of the performance, "I never knew you could perform so well."

"Of course not," she said softly as she touched his forehead with her forefinger. "It's all those books you read."

The next day Senator Gaius called his daughter to his study.

"Junia, I am pleased to report that you have most favorably impressed Assistant Prefect Quintus." She could tell from his formal tone that he had something important to say. He always did that, as if he were on the Senate floor . . . and it always secretly amused her.

"He would like to continue seeing you when we return to Rome."

---

* A musical instrument resembling a harp, only of smaller size.

Junia smiled self-consciously. She had had many suitors in Rome before, but her father had not considered any of them worthy. She waited in silence, looking into her father's eyes.

"Junia, though perhaps it's too early to say, I think he would be a good husband for you. He's noble, a bit conceited perhaps, but . . ."

"Father, say no more. I liked him too. I have to admit that I didn't really want to impress anybody last night. I simply played the lyre with some tunes that Marcia taught me, and everybody seemed to enjoy it."

Junia chuckled softly, threw her father a kiss, and left his study. She was very anxious to tell Marcia everything, so much seemed to be happening. She began counting the days until her friend's arrival.

XI.

Three days before Marcia's scheduled arrival, Junia had her family humming with activity. She had written a small play about a corrupt Corinthian judge, which she knew Marcia would especially like. She double-checked some of the jokes and the plays on words with Cynthia. Everyone in the family had a part, including her father. Senator Gaius was at first reluctant, but since the part had a certain dignity, he accepted. He was so pleased with his recent good fortune that he found it hard to say no.

The day finally came for Marcia's arrival. Junia got up early that day to make sure that her chamber was in perfect condition. She had the slaves put the best linens on the bed, and Junia herself brought some flowers that she knew Marcia would like. The day progressed, and her dear friend did not come. By nightfall, Junia was quite worried.

"Father, could she have been robbed on the way?"

"Hardly likely, not with a strong force of Diodorus's servants accompanying her. Be patient, Daughter; tomorrow we shall see."

Junia hardly slept that night. She had a lively imagination that kept inventing all kinds of mishaps that could have occurred. Maybe she was sick; maybe there were riots in Rome; maybe she changed her mind. In the end she began to feel angry with Marcia. The least she could have done was to send a messenger, if there were some problem.

By noon the next day, Junia asked her father to send a messenger to Diodorus's house. The Senator did not think it unreasonable and commissioned his Macedonian slave Fabian to take one of their swiftest horses to the capitol.

"Don't worry, Daughter," Gaius said. "Fabian will probably come across Marcia's train on the road."

The next day, toward dusk, Fabian returned. Junia was waiting for him in front of the villa, and after he dismounted she ran up to him. "What news, Fabian?" she said anxiously.

Fabian looked away from her for a moment and shook his head slowly.

"I'm sorry, Miss Junia."

"Sorry? About what?" She was almost shouting at him.

"Miss Junia," the man said slowly, as if weighing each word, "Miss Marcia and her father have been killed in the Flavian Amphitheatre. They were Christians."

Junia stared at him for some time. She could not believe what she had just heard. She refused to believe it.

"I went to their home," the messenger continued, "and the new owners told me. I also read the list of events in the amphitheatre. Diodorus and his daughter were executed on July 18th for the treason of being Christians. Their bodies were taken by members of their sect to some burial ground outside of the city. That is all I know, Miss Junia. I am very sorry."

Junia fell to her knees and leaned her head against a large olive tree near the house. Her whole body was shaking, and she was sobbing violently. The wiry, athletic slave from northern Greece could barely hear her, as she kept mumbling the same words again and again.

"My best friend, my best friend, the best friend I ever had . . ." And then suddenly she cried out furiously, beating the tree trunk with both of her fists. "O you gods, I hate you! I hate all of you! Have you no pity on us?"

She made an effort to regain her composure, though she continued to tremble. She realized that she was in the presence of a slave and had to maintain her dignity. She rose to her feet slowly.

"You may tell my father, Fabian. Thank you," she said softly.

As soon as he had left, she ran to a nearby field, to a small meadow where she liked to go in her free moments. And there she wept, more than she had ever wept before.

XII.

The remaining days at the family villa were miserable for her. For several days she refused to eat; she lost her delightful way of teasing people and of telling funny stories. She did not want to sing. The other members of the family tried to console her. Her mother kept speaking to her about how handsome Quintus was, and how he would bring even more fame to the family. She reminded her that she was considered to be one of the most talented girls in Rome and that it was foolish to shed so many tears for a dead friend.

Marcus was more abstract in his approach. He could understand his sister's initial grief, but thought it was a real weakness to continue so long in the same situation. After giving her some general appeals about the value of fond memories, and a kind of universal humanitarian experience, he did not press the subject further. His respect for his sister's mental acumen began to diminish. He reasoned that it was the weakness of the female sex to let the emotions of a single friendship so damage one's internal harmony. Needless to say, Junia's father thought the same about her moodiness.

Toward the end of the summer Junia approached her brother in a rather melancholic but reflective frame of mind.

"Marcus," she said gravely, "do you remember that a few months ago you told me that you were going to investigate this sect called Christianity? You mentioned something about a man named Justin, and his theories. What did you find out?"

Junia's brother was glad to see her interest in some outside subject and quickly offered his opinion and conversation.

"To tell you the truth, I was quite impressed with Justin. I think he has a great career ahead of him. He's quite brilliant, especially when he expounds his theory of how Greek philosophy has been leading to Christianity for centuries."

Junia looked at him with great attention and curiosity.

"Yes, but did he explain to you what Christians believe?"

Marcus waved his hand as if trying to dismiss or ridicule something.

"Oh, he gave me some rather involved description of it. It was a bit too much for me. People rising from the dead, miraculous cures, and other such things. Oh, yes; he also mentioned something else: the importance of loving one another. This Galilean carpenter taught that in a special way."

As Marcus spoke, Junia felt herself becoming more and more interested.

"Yes, yes. That sounds right," she said anxiously. "Go on. What more did he say about loving one another?"

"Junia, why are you so interested all of a sudden in Christianity?" Then he paused for a moment and looked back at her inquisitively. "Wait, of course I know. It's because your friend Marcia was a Christian."

Junia turned away from him for a moment and passed her hand over her smooth dark hair.

"Yes," she said softly, and then quietly left the room.

That night Senator Gaius called for his daughter. He was quite disturbed at her prolonged reaction to her friend's death, and he thought it most unbecoming to be so disconsolate. His pride was hurt, since he had always considered Junia to be a sensible person. She was obviously unable to control her emotions. Furthermore she had been imprudent in befriending a Christian; with more foresight and reflection she could have avoided it altogether. He wanted to have a good talk with her.

He began very gently. "Junia, dear daughter, why are you so sad?"

"Father," Junia looked at him earnestly, "I have lost a great treasure, someone who truly cared for me, as I cared for her. And I don't know why it had to happen; it seems terribly unfair."

The Senator stood up and approached his daughter; he took her hand in his and patted it gently.

"Your friend and her father were Christians. That was their great mistake. They may have had certain qualities that you admired, but you cannot forget the great error they made. To be a Christian is tantamount to treason."

Junia's eyes began to moisten. "But Father, I knew Marcia and her father. They were good, loyal citizens of Rome. They did not plot treason against the Emperor, or anyone else."

"Ah!" the Senator exclaimed, as if he had some special knowledge that his daughter did not have. "But they have secret meetings! You didn't know about that, did you? And in those meetings who knows what they do or say? I even heard that they drink human blood. How do you know that their kindness to you was not a mere cover for their treason?"

Junia nodded her head slightly. She had heard similar things about the Christians.

"Yes, that's true. I suppose it's a possibility, but . . ." she began to speak haltingly as if trying to control something welling up inside of her, "but I am sure that their goodness was genuine; they weren't thinking of themselves, or their own gain. Oh, Father," she cried out, "I don't know what to think. All I know is that she was wonderful, and I loved her as if she were my sister!"

Senator Gaius smiled faintly, wisely. . . .

"It will pass, Junia. I don't doubt that Diodorus and his daughter had good qualities that impressed you. Probably some business competitor of Diodorus denounced him as a Christian, in order to ruin him. By force of law a trial would have to be held. He and his daughter should have offered wine and incense to the statue of the Emperor and renounced their superstition. Actually this Emperor has been very lenient with Christians compared to others, like Nero and Domitian."

"Listen, Junia. Here is my advice to you as a father. Try to forget this girl. Take what is good, take what she gave you, and live your own life. You are a talented young woman and have a marvellous future ahead of you. You have a family that cares for you. Don't let a past experience chain you to the earth when you can soar like an eagle in Rome. There's so much waiting for you, my daughter, and you're still young."

Junia smiled appreciatively. Her father's words did much to calm her, and she resolved to stop thinking about the situation any further. Yet in her heart she knew that she could never forget Marcia. She was troubled and could not understand why.

XIII.

Upon returning to Rome, the Senator and his family became the center of attention. Word spread quickly that the Emperor had encouraged him to present himself as a candidate for the consulship, which was tantamount to appointing him. Gaius had many speaking engagements and many dinner invitations. Days went by without his family's seeing him.

There were also social obligations to fulfill. Even Marcus, who disliked dinners and games in general, had to attend several of them. He also noticed, a bit cynically, how some of his peers began to listen to his theories more readily, and even to applaud some of his wilder ideas. He liked to joke with his sister a lot about that. "And so truth is once again sacrificed on the altar of adulation," he quipped.

Aurelia could not be more pleased. She loved the attention she was getting and accepted invitation after invitation, to the point of becoming ill. More than anything, she appreciated the frequent remarks about her beauty; when someone compared her with her lovely daughter, she was particularly touched. She spent long hours before the mirror, having her hair fixed according to the most recent fashions. She even convinced Gaius to hire a certain Egyptian cosmetician to visit their mansion twice a week, in order to attend to herself and Junia. "After all," she told him, "Junia and I are part of your household image." Gaius smiled at that; he thought it was the wisest thing she had ever said.

Junia did not care much for the cosmeticians. She found them conceited—and at times ridiculous. They brought their own servants with them, whom they treated like dirt, though they were extremely polite with her. She much preferred to have Cynthia do her hair and only employed the Egyptians when a very important event was coming.

Junia had many suitors, who called on her constantly. They were mostly sons of senators or rich merchants, though occasionally she would receive a visit from a foreign dignitary as well. She tried to be cordial to them all, but at times she could not resist the chance to tease them. It was easy to tease them, she thought, since they all seemed to take themselves so seriously.

Of all her suitors the one she favored most was Quintus. He was rather proud and self-sufficient, but he had the modesty to recognize that much of his good fortune was owed to his good birth. He was strong and probably the most athletic of all her suitors, since he had seen active duty and was also in daily training as a Praetorian Guard. He had a certain appreciation for literature and philosophy, which she felt was not feigned, as in most of her other suitors.

One morning, about a month after their return from Latium, Junia had to accept an invitation to dinner at Agrippina's mansion. Though she did not care to go, she was happy that at least she did not have to go to the games as before. Some of the wealthiest and most influential young people of Rome were expected.

All eyes seemed to focus upon her as she entered the atrium.

"Junia, dearest," Livia cried out loudly, and ran to embrace her. "Just as lovely as ever, and with hardly any makeup! You must tell me your secret some time." Livia kissed Junia on the cheek, but to Junia it seemed more like a bite than a kiss, and she drew away from her instinctively.

"Come now, daughter of Gaius, you must join in our conversation. We were just talking about that most dreadful topic . . . Christians!"

Junia bit her lip. She felt at home with practically any subject but that. Before the summer she could speak confidently, even wittily, about Christians . . . basing herself on her father's opinions, and what her peers were saying. But once she had discovered that Marcia was a Christian, her ideas became confused, because she knew that Marcia was not ignorant, blasphemous, or immoral. She decided to keep quiet, even at the risk of appearing dull or uninformed.

"I heard that they tie dogs to lamps," began one rather short fellow standing next to Livia. "Then they whip them, and all the lights go out. You can imagine what happens next."

There were some knowing laughs at that point.

"So that's how they practice their mutual love," one young woman chimed in.

"The worst of all is that they're so obstinate," said another. "They won't give up their faith in this dead Galilean, Jesus, even to save their lives."

"Yes, as a matter of fact there was a Christian just two months ago, a fellow named Diodorus from Corinth, who refused to offer wine and incense to the statue of the Emperor. He was doing very well for himself here in Rome, though he was not a citizen."

Up to this point Junia had been listening calmly. But upon hearing Diodorus's name, she immediately stiffened. Trying to remain calm and nonchalant, she asked, "What did they do to him?"

"Crucified him in the Flavian Amphitheatre. Upside down. I was there," said a rather tall fellow with a thin beard, standing in the back.

"Upside down, eh?" someone else asked. "You'd think they'd be a little more original. They've been doing that to Christians since Nero's time."

"Oh, they were original alright," the narrator continued. "You should have seen what they did to his daughter."

There were a few whistles in the group, and some obscene gestures from a few of the young gentlemen who were trying to guess what they had done to her.

"Oh, no," the narrator laughed, "it was much better than that. First they covered her back with pitch, and then as the silly girl kept singing something about 'Jesus' and 'Christ,' they set her on fire. The crowds were howling with laughter. Afterward the lions came and made quick work of her."

Junia was visibly trembling at this point. Her face was very pale. She had to be absolutely sure. Almost inaudibly she asked, "And what did the girl look like?"

The young Roman stared back at her with a kind of lustfulness in his eyes. "Quite plain. Short, stubby, with red curly hair. She couldn't hold a candle to you, Junia."

After the dinner, when she returned home, Junia went straight to her room. She spent the rest of the day, and all of that night, in anguish. She was sorry, not so much for herself now, but for Marcia, who had been so kind and had never harmed anyone, not even by word. She remembered how good the Corinthian girl had been to her on many occasions and how she had helped her to be cheerful and thoughtful. She owed her so much. It was a horrible injustice that she had to die in that way.

She rose from her bed and lit a small chamber torch. With its light she could see her reflection on a small glass window. Her clear blue eyes had become clouded with tears, and her long black hair was tossed about wildly. "Aye," she muttered to herself, "and they say I'm beautiful. Compared to Marcia, I think I'm very ugly." She pushed back her cheeks with her hands and made the ugliest face that she could . . . then stuck out her tongue at her own reflection.

She kept thinking about the cruel conversation at Livia's that afternoon. "And they call themselves the high society of Rome; they're disgusting!" She knelt down beside her bed and struck her fist on top of her fine cedar night table. She felt hatred for the people who had executed her best friend. She wished them far worse deaths than Marcia's. They deserved it a thousand, thousand times.

Marcia had made the great mistake of being a Christian. Junia had heard so many conflicting things about Christians, that she did not know what to believe. Certainly all the members of her family, and all her peers, were against them. And yet this girl and her father were the most gentle and loveable persons that she had known. Junia halted for a moment in her thoughts. "Wait! Was she really a Christian? She never really said anything about it. Perhaps she was duped into it by others, or her father, Diodorus, was falsely accused. No intelligent person would give up his or her life so easily. Marcia was surely smart enough to avoid that," Junia reflected.

Her head began to ache. She was convinced that she would never know the real answer. All she knew was that there was little love in Rome and that in her own soul she felt a great bitterness.

THE FINDING OF LOVE

I.

The next morning Cynthia entered Junia's chamber shortly after dawn.

"You have a woman visitor, Miss. She didn't want to come into the atrium but is waiting for you outside the front door."

"A visitor so early? That is strange. Did she give a name?"

"No, Miss."

"What does she look like?"

"She's an older woman, in common clothes. She has a Gallic accent."

Junia got up and slipped on her tunic and sandals. The atrium was already filled with Gaius's assistants, who were especially busy these days. The Senator was giving orders to each one. Bombolinus spotted Junia walking through the atrium, bowed deeply and hailed her. "Good morning, Miss Junia, daughter of Gaius! May the gods bring you a most handsome, and wealthy, husband."

Junia stared at him coldly. She was in no mood for silly outbursts.

The lady waiting for her was tall, with a frayed hood, and somewhat of a stoop. Her face was hidden by a veil. Junia extended her hand, which she took quickly while bowing low. The older woman's hand was trembling quite a bit, and it felt cold and sweaty in Junia's soft palm.

"Who are you?" the Roman girl asked. "And what is your message?"

"Begging your pardon, Miss. My mistress asked me to give this to you personally. I'm sorry that I have taken so long. But I was afraid."

And after saying these words, she produced a scroll with a dark red seal of wax, placed it in Junia's hands, and ran down the hill. Junia shouted after her for her name, but it was too late.

"Shall I try to catch her, Miss?" asked Cynthia.

"No, no. Let's see what this is first."

Junia opened the seal and immediately detected the handwriting that had entertained and cheered her so many times before. It was Marcia's.

Junia felt as if she were going to faint; she leaned on the front column for support.

"Miss," Cynthia asked quickly, "is there anything wrong? Do you feel ill?"

"Help me to my chamber, Cynthia," her mistress answered in an almost inaudible voice. "I want to be alone for a while."

As soon as she was alone in her room, Junia opened the scroll and began to read:

My dear friend Junia,

How unhappy I am that I will not be able to visit you and your family this summer. I had something very important to tell you, but now I must write it.

I really don't know how to begin. It's about love, the greatest love in the world, which has been my joy for many years, and my father's as well. You see, dear Junia, we are Christians. I hope that this does not make you hate me. That was what I wanted to tell you that day I was so solemn, but I couldn't find the words, or the courage, to do so.

Now I have the courage, but it seems too late, because my father and I are going to die for our faith. Some friends in Rome have suggested that we offer wine and incense to Caesar's statue, but we could never do that because it would be a betrayal of Jesus, who is the only hope of our lives. Jesus has made my father and me wonderfully happy; we're even happy now, though we are going to die.

Can you understand that, dear Junia? I pray to my God that you can! You must think that I am crazy, but to love and serve Jesus Christ is the most marvelous thing in the world. He gives the soul a strength and a sweetness beyond compare. Oh Junia, I feel so bad that I didn't tell you about our faith earlier. It would have made you so happy; please forgive me.

Dear Miss Nobli-nubli, I have tears in my eyes now . . . and it's all your fault! I hope that they don't fall on this good scroll my father bought for me. You should see him, Junia. He's so brave. Really, he's helping me to be strong right now. This morning we prayed to our God for you and your father, and mother, and brother, and—Oh Junia, I can't hide it any longer—I prayed that some day you too could know and love our Savior Jesus Christ. That is my greatest, most secret wish.

Junia, they've come to take us to prison now. I'm leaving this letter with Scintilla, one of our servants who is a Christian. You met her once or twice in your visits here; do you remember? She will give it to you as soon as she can.

My dearest friend, I have to go now. I hope my death is quick, but if it isn't, I'll offer it for you. Goodbye, Junia.

Marcia

Junia read the letter four times, trying to savor every word, thought, and sentiment expressed in it. She was amazed that she was not shedding one tear, though Marcia seemed to be crying when she wrote it. Within her soul she sensed that something profound was happening to her, though she could not explain it. It seemed that suddenly a great weight had been lifted from her.

II.

That night Junia resolved to visit Marcia's tomb and, if she could, to learn more about Christianity. She felt that she owed that to Marcia, since she was the best friend she ever had, and since she had shared her intimate secret with her before she died. She doubted that she would ever become a Christian herself, but she thought it a duty of justice to visit her tomb.

It would be hard. She knew that the Christians buried their dead in the catacombs and occasionally had ceremonies there. The catacombs were located on the outskirts of Rome, but she had no idea where her friend was buried in them. Furthermore, her father would never permit her to visit such a place; he would be scandalized and horrified, she was sure of it. To honor the burial place of a friend was an ancient Roman custom, but if that friend were a Christian . . .

She had no one to turn to. Cynthia was very good, but she was also quite anti-Christian. She would never understand what she was doing and might even tell her father. As far as she could tell, none of their house slaves were Christians either; the Senator would not have allowed that.

She resolved to take a tremendous chance. She would try to leave the house disguised and to make her bed in such a way that it seemed she was sleeping in it. She knew of an old servants' exit that no one used, on the east side of the mansion. That evening she would leave the house dressed as a common plebeian woman; she had the wardrobe that she had prepared for the play in the villa.

As the sun set, she felt particularly nervous and began to waver in her plan. It was the first time that she was ever leaving her father's house alone and unaccompanied. A sudden plea rose up in her heart; she found herself praying, almost instinctively, "Jesus Christ, Marcia's god, help me!"

Leaving the mansion was the hardest part. Once on the street, jostled by the crowds, she was just one more. Most were hurrying to their homes, pushing each other. It was the first time she had ever walked the street with the crowds. The sweat, the foul words, and the pushing nauseated her. But she kept walking on, keeping her face well covered with a veil. She was glad her disguise was working so well, but she also felt humiliated. Finally, after walking for nearly an hour, she arrived to the area of the catacombs, across the Tiber near the Vatican hills. It was almost night. Though it was known that most Christian meetings took place in private homes, sometimes Christians would go to these underground passages to bury the dead or to pray there for them. Junia was hoping that she would be fortunate enough to join such a group. She hid behind a couple of trees to observe who would come up the road. A horse-drawn wagon came at first, probably bearing a rich merchant to his country villa. A long time passed and no one else came. Junia began to lose hope. But just as she was about to turn back, she saw a small procession of men and women, in groups of four or five, walking cautiously along the road and speaking quietly. She followed the third such group, from a distance, until they entered an underground cave. She paused for a moment, bit her upper lip for courage, and walked toward the cave entrance.

The guard was a tall black man, probably from one of the northern African provinces. He had a faint smile on his face, but also an attitude of caution. "Sister, do you bring peace?" he asked as he pointed the torch in her direction.

Junia did not know what to answer. She suspected that there must be some kind of a password involved, which of course she didn't know. She decided that the best course of action would be to state the purpose of her visit, simply and directly.

"I . . . am a friend of Marcia, daughter of Diodorus. I am not a Christian but would like to see her tomb if it is here."

The guard looked quite disconcerted and asked her to wait there for a moment. He came back with someone that Junia recognized immediately; it was Scintilla, the servant who had brought her Marcia's letter on that very morning. Though she had worn a veil, Junia recognized her by her eyes and high forehead, and also by her slight stoop.

But the woman had no way of recognizing her. "Miss," she said with a great gentleness in her voice, "kindly let me see your face, so that I may know who you are."

Junia pushed aside her veil, and Scintilla gasped audibly. Then after a moment, she smiled.

"Yes," the older woman said softly, and then turning to the guard she added, "It's alright to let her pass. I'll take responsibility for her."

III.

The catacomb was very damp, and Junia shivered as they entered. They went down a few steps into a narrow passageway; at one point Junia had to stoop to avoid hitting her head. There was a lighted torch at the end of the passageway, and Junia could hear men and women singing together in the distance.

"What are they singing?" Junia whispered to her companion, who was leading the way.

"They're celebrating the Eucharist," the older woman answered. "You'll see them as we pass by that opening."

When they arrived to the place of the torch, Junia could see, about thirty feet to the right, a group of nearly twenty people, both men and women, kneeling in front of a rough stone altar. A man was lifting some pieces of bread, as if offering them to the people. The daughter of Gaius stared at them, fascinated. This was not at all what she had heard about Christian gatherings. The people were very clean, and quite decently dressed. Most of them seemed to be servants or freemen from the lower class, though she did notice two men with togas and three women with noble stolas.* They all seemed to be concentrating very much on the prayers and the bread.

Junia felt a hand on her shoulder. "This is called the

---

* Long one-piece garments worn by Roman matrons (upper class).

Eucharist. But this isn't what you came to see, is it?" Scintilla asked her softly.

Junia looked at Scintilla; she was a tall woman, with well-formed features, perhaps sixty years of age. What most struck Junia were her eyes; they seemed almost sad, though the lips were smiling.

"No," said Junia. "I've come to visit Marcia's tomb."

Scintilla took her down another passageway, this time with a small torch in her hand. They came to a kind of small open area, not as large as the previous one, which had several tombs in the wall, capped by semi-circular niches in the wall. Each tomb had an inscription. Some of them were in Latin, some in Greek:

> *"May he sleep in the peace of Christ."*
> *"May she rest in the Lord."*
> *"May the eternal light shine upon her."*
> *"Peace to you."*

After looking at several, Junia asked which one was Marcia's. Scintilla did not answer right away but encouraged her to keep looking. Junia passed the torch in front of each one until she came to a tombstone very close to the ground, and quite new looking. Unlike the others, it had an image etched into the stone slab; it looked like a ship moving ahead at full sail. Underneath the image Junia could read the following words in Greek: *"Your ship has come. Sail on, Marcia, sail on."*

The Roman girl did not understand. She stooped nearly to the ground, kissed the tomb, and spent a few minutes in silence looking down. She felt confused, since she only knew prayers to the Olympian gods, which she had learned at some official state ceremonies. But she never really believed in them and was a kind of skeptic about the entire religion, like many educated young people of her time. She could only say softly: "Marcia, you were my dearest friend. I wish you were alive again with me."

She rose slowly and turned around. Her companion was sitting on one of the stone steps. "Forgive me, Miss, I'm not as young as I used to be."

Junia went to her and sat beside her.

"I remember your face, Scintilla; you used to serve in the kitchen at Diodorus's home. I want to thank you for bringing that letter to me; I know that it was a big risk for you."

"It was a bigger risk for you to come here, Miss Junia," the older woman said as she touched Junia's hand. "You're a very brave girl."

"She was braver," Junia replied simply as she motioned toward Marcia's tomb. Then she grasped Scintilla's hand warmly within hers. "Please tell me something about her religion. For instance, why does it say on her tomb: Sail on? To where?"

"I don't know if you would understand, Miss Junia."

"I would like to try. And you don't have to call me Miss Junia. Just call me Junia."

Scintilla then explained the concept of heaven to her, as clearly as she could. A place of great love and peace, where only the just could enter.

"And is that where Marcia is now?"

"I am sure she is," Scintilla said softly.

"And why was she always so happy about things? That is what I most remember about her."

Scintilla rose to her feet slowly. She took the small torch and walked a few paces to the right, to a large fresco painting that Junia had not been able to distinguish clearly. With Scintilla's light, she was able to see the image of a young man, very handsome and cheerful looking, holding a sheep upon his shoulders.

"Why was she always so happy?" Scintilla repeated her young friend's question. "Because she loved the Good Shepherd with her whole mind and strength, and followed his commandments faithfully. She was faithful to him until the end, even when they took her and . . ."

Junia looked expectantly at the woman from Gaul, but her voice was trembling. Junia could see tears welling up in her eyes. "Even . . . ," Scintilla continued with a halting voice, "even when they burned her, she was singing to him, for all to hear."

Then she began to tremble violently and couldn't speak anymore.

Junia walked up to her and embraced her, kissing her on both sides of her face, and together both women wept for several moments.

"Scintilla," Junia said softly after a while, "I want to learn about Jesus and his teachings. Could you teach me?"

"I would be very happy to do so," Scintilla replied, wiping away her tears. "But it would be very dangerous. You shouldn't come back here again."

"No," Junia reflected. "No, not here, but perhaps you could come to me . . . at my home for instance."

Scintilla looked astonished. "At your home? That would be impossible. . . . We would both be discovered, for sure."

Her young companion's eyes began to sparkle, as if she had received a delightful challenge, or as if she were playing an exciting game.

"But of course you can come to my home! I shall hire you as my tutor!"

Scintilla smiled. It seemed as if she were hearing Marcia again, with all of her energy and wit, instead of her Roman friend.

"But Miss, I am old and am nothing but a kitchen slave. People would ask how I could teach you anything. They will surely suspect something."

Junia looked down toward Marcia's tomb and reflected for a moment.

"You are from Gaul, aren't you?"

"Yes, from the central part."

"Well, you can teach me the Gallic language and customs. One of our emperors was so interested in your people that he wrote a long account about you. I am sure that I can convince my father to let you teach me."

Scintilla shook her head uneasily. "What if someone should discover that I'm teaching you Christianity, and not Gallic."

"Don't worry, Scintilla. I'll study Gallic, too; in that way nobody will suspect. You can teach me many words and phrases. Come now . . . ," the Roman girl's clear blue eyes lit up almost mischievously. . . . "Say yes."

Scintilla nodded and smiled. "Yes," she said almost inaudibly. "Yes, dear Junia, yes."

IV.

Rome at night was an inferno of screeching carts, shouts, and curses. In Augustus's time all merchant traffic had been outlawed during the day, to allow free transit for Rome's five hundred thousand pedestrians. But the cost of that was dear. Except for those privileged to live on one of the seven hills, in a mansion, the other inhabitants of Rome had to put up with a constant din at night, often occurring in front of their shops and tenements.

In the catacombs a Christian family had offered to drive Junia back to the city. There was room in their cart for one more person. The family drove in silence, for which Junia was grateful; she did not want to converse so as to identify herself, and she kept on her veil. The mother and father were in the front, and she sat between the two children—a girl of ten and a boy of twelve. They were obviously plebeians, probably owners of a small fish or wine shop.

Junia was amazed at the father's patience and even temper—given the furious pace of the carts and wagons all around them. He spoke not a word and maneuvered his cart well. Junia could tell that he had great dexterity, from all the times that he had to drive his products to the city at night.

As they were leaving Via Appia, they were faced with a

long line of carts, all trying to get into the city. At one point, about five carts ahead of them, an apple vender was trying to pass a bigger wagon, with very little success. As he was trying to get by, the bigger cart bumped into him and forced the apple vender with his cart into a side embankment. Almost all of his produce fell to the ground. The vender leaped from the cart and began to run after the bigger wagon, cursing violently. He was unable to catch it and returned to his disabled cart shaking his head and stamping his foot to the ground. One by one, he began to pick up the apples.

It was hard not to laugh at the scene. Junia herself was giggling, and she could hear soft laughter in the front seat. "Quite a disaster," the father was saying. But then she heard something, from the same manly voice, that completely surprised her. "Let's stop and help him."

Junia was not prepared for that. If she had her way, they would have continued ahead like all the other carts. She felt cold and was anxious to be home. As far as she could see, the ill-fated driver had merited his fate anyway. Why did this family have to stop to help him? Did they know him?

But she kept quiet, knowing that she too was being helped by them. The paterfamilias* pulled his cart up deftly behind the vendor's, moving it out of the way of the wagons behind him. He and his two children quickly stepped out of the cart and began to help the distraught man in gathering his apples, after assuring him that they were there to help, not to take anything. He seemed incredulous at first but then seemed quite grateful for the assistance. The two children were laughing, while their mother remained in the front seat holding the reins of the horse.

Junia couldn't resist asking her, "Why are they doing that? Do they know that vendor?"

The mother turned toward Junia, with a surprised look on

* Head of the family, with authority and custody of the home.

her face, but she said nothing. Junia then remembered something that Marcus had told her about Christian belief: their idea of loving others. She also remembered—how could she forget?—how Marcia had visited her when she was sick and even how kind Scintilla had just been to her. She didn't know what to do, as if she had just been placed in another world, with another set of rules. She felt awkward and somewhat humiliated.

"Miss," a child's voice said. "Can you help us?" It was the little girl, who had walked back to the cart. She was obviously getting tired, and there were many apples on the ground.

Junia hesitated for a moment but then stepped down gracefully from the back seat and began to pick up apples with the little girl. Many of them had already been crushed by carts, and some of them had fallen into horse dung on the side of the road. The young aristocratic woman made a face but kept working. "And all of this," she thought, "for someone I don't even know. How can it be?" Then she laughed out loud but didn't know why. She thought of Marcia laughing and blowing gold dust off her hair. "*Nobli-nubli,*" she whispered to herself as she picked up more apples.

When they had finished, they continued on their journey. The family left her close to the Senator's mansion, at the foot of the hill. She thanked them, and after they had gone, she began to walk up the long entranceway, lined with poplar trees. She was glad that only a few cats were to be seen, but she was afraid that they might meow and wake up the servants. Instinctively she prayed, "Jesus, help that all be quiet." Finally, walking very silently, she managed to enter the house through the unused servants' entrance and crept into her room.

She removed her plebeian clothes and patted them. "You did good work tonight," she joked. Then she left a note asking Cynthia not to wake her until midday. As she lay down, she thought of all the wonderful things that she had witnessed that evening, including the apples. She never thought that she could come so close to Christianity in just one evening. As she drifted into sleep, she felt happier than she had felt in a long time.

V.

Scintilla began to see Junia at Senator Gaius's mansion three days each week. In private conversations she explained the basic Christian belief in the Holy Trinity: in God the Father, Creator of all things; in God the Son, who became a man to save all people from sin; in God the Holy Spirit, who was the living force of the Church that Jesus had founded.

At times the former kitchen slave felt embarrassed, because she did not have the vocabulary to express profound ideas, nor could she speak the educated Latin of her young student . . . but she gave Junia many examples drawn from her life and that of others—especially of how the Holy Spirit would encourage and inspire people.

"For instance," she told Junia one day, "we believe that our bodies are temples of the Holy Spirit and that it is wrong to violate them . . . by eating or drinking too much, or by lustful actions. Jesus said, 'Blessed are the pure of heart, for they shall see God.'"

At that point Junia asked her some very direct and personal questions about being chaste, which the older woman answered clearly and without hesitation. Sexual relations were meant for marriage, she said, and to have sex or seek its pleasure outside of marriage was seriously wrong and prohibited by the Lord. People who committed these sins were in danger of being lost, unless they repented. And then she added that the Holy Spirit would always help those who sincerely wanted to lead a clean life, despite the bad example of other people and the temptations of the world.

Junia had other questions that she wanted to ask about sexual matters, but she was too embarrassed to ask them then. On another occasion, however, she found her courage and asked her teacher about certain things that had been bothering her.

"What about lustful thoughts and desires, Scintilla. Is it wrong to think of them, even if a person doesn't do them?"

"Immoral thoughts or desires can occur to us," Scintilla said simply, "but it's wrong to consent to them within our mind or heart. Because Jesus said, 'The man who looks at a woman with lust has already committed adultery with her in his heart.'"

Junia softly whistled to herself when she heard that and nodded her head. She had always suspected that it was so, though she had never put it into words. Most of the philosophers that she and Marcus had read were very indulgent about sexual affairs; they would lose popularity otherwise. But if a person was to avoid immoral actions like adultery and fornication, then certainly lustful thoughts would also be wrong. She was grateful for the good training that her father had given her, especially the importance of self-control and discipline. But for him, and for the Stoics in general, the real reason for chastity was self-perfection. Scintilla was saying something different; she was saying that the real reason for chastity was love, above all love for God. Junia was deeply moved by that and would think about it often in the days to come.

Another thing that Junia asked was how Marcia and her father had become Christians.

"Diodorus's father was converted by Paul of Tarsus, in one of his journeys to Corinth. All his sons and daughters followed his path; when Diodorus and Marcia came to Rome, they simply continued to practice what they had learned in Corinth. I never met Marcia's mother, who was also a Christian. She died when Marcia was three."

"Marcia's mother! What a wonderful woman she must have been. . . ."

"All I know is that she was a very good singer."

"That certainly makes sense. But what about you, Scintilla? When did you become a Christian?"

"Oh, Junia, you're a tricky one. You want me to show my age."

"No, not at all," Junia protested good-naturedly. "For me you'll always be young. But tell me, how did you become a Christian?"

Scintilla smiled somewhat shyly and squinted her eyes. "I was a hard one. I was taken from Gaul to Rome in my early twenties and ended up working as a kitchen slave in the house of a wealthy quaestor, during Trajan's reign. One of my kitchen companions, a Syrian girl, began to tell me about Christianity and how it had changed her life. She was from Antioch. She wanted me to go to one of their meetings and to take instruction."

"Did you go?"

"Not at first; she seemed too enthusiastic about it, too anxious for me to go. I was interested though and tried to learn more about it from other slaves who were Christians. Frankly it was hard for me to decide. I admired them for their courage and their charity, but they seemed to be doing something impossible. It was so dangerous, and everybody spoke badly of them."

"Like today," Junia commented.

"Yes, it's about the same situation, though this emperor seems more tolerant. At any rate, I was about to drop the idea of becoming a Christian, until I saw Ignatius, who was a bishop."

"A bishop? What's a bishop?"

"Oh, we haven't gotten to that in our lessons yet. For now, let's say that a bishop is the one in charge of a large group of Christians."

"Like a commander over a legion?"

"Something like that, but not quite so military. At any rate, Ignatius was the bishop of Antioch and very outspoken in his faith. He had refused to offer incense to the Emperor's statue. When they brought him to Rome, he was over eighty years old. You should have seen him, Junia. He was so courageous! Just before they sent him to the lions, he prayed for his executioners, and he said a prayer that I will never forget."

"What was that?"

"He said, 'I am the wheat of God, and by the teeth of wild beasts I am ground so that I may become the pure bread of Christ.'"

The Roman girl's bright eyes widened.

"Did he really say that before he was to die? He had an unusual sense of humor!"

"It wasn't humor—it was the grace of God in his heart. When I saw him, I realized that Christianity must be something very profound. At that moment I resolved to learn more and began to go for instruction at the home of a Christian merchant. Within a year I was baptized; it was the happiest moment of my life."

"Baptized? That's another word that you haven't explained to me. If you don't go faster, I'll have to fire you!" Junia replied as she gave her a playful shove.

VI.

In the months before Gaius's appointment as consul, Junia was the most sought after woman in Rome. There was a constant flow of suitors; some of them very elevated in the government, and some even very close friends of Caesar.

Quintus began to despair that he would ever obtain her. She was by far the most lovely and intelligent girl that he had ever met, but most of Junia's suitors were of higher rank than he, and Quintus feared that for political reasons he would not be chosen. Being a forthright and sincere person, he made an appointment with the Senator and discussed the matter thoroughly. He repeated that he would be very honored to be able to marry his daughter and could provide very well for her. The Senator did not commit himself; he said he would discuss the matter with Junia and would give her answer in due time.

The following evening Gaius called his daughter to his study.

"I have excellent news, Junia. My consulship is almost a certainty now. Most of the political arrangements have been made."

"That's wonderful, Father!" Junia exclaimed as she ran up to him and held his hand warmly. "With all the work that you've been doing, you certainly deserve it."

"I have you to thank, and your mother and brother as well. You have projected a most favorable image. Above all, you, Junia. At times I think the Emperor himself would propose to you if he could get away with it."

Junia blushed for a moment. She had always been self-conscious about compliments. These particular days she was trying to take Scintilla's advice and not give them importance; she had learned that everything, including beauty and talent, was a free gift from the one God.

"At any rate," the Senator continued, "there's an important question that we should answer as soon as possible. Junia, be very frank with me. Of all the suitors that are seeing you now, whom do you prefer?"

Junia smiled gratefully at her father; she knew of many Roman girls her age who had not been consulted before their marriage.

"Father, of them all I prefer Quintus. But I will do what is best for you and for our family. The only thing I ask . . ." Junia's voice suddenly faltered and she lowered her glance.

"Yes, go ahead, my dearest," Gaius encouraged.

"The only thing I ask, Father, is that he be a real man," and Junia's voice became firm again.

"Why, aren't all of your suitors men?"

Junia shook her head.

"Not really. Some of those with a lot of money and good family connections . . . could not be anybody's husband in the true sense of the word. Two of them have no character at all, and one of them . . . ," Junia frowned and turned her head away, ". . . is strange."

Gaius began to laugh out loud. He was not given to laughter because of his Stoic upbringing, but his daughter's candor appealed to him.

"Junia, those are probably the most honest words that I have heard in many months. I agree with you. Though he is not the richest or most well-connected suitor, Quintus is the best choice."

Gaius looked at the gentle smile that was spreading across his daughter's lips. He had been very busy for the last few months and had not noticed her as much. But now it seemed to him that Junia had become more affectionate and loveable than he could ever remember. Though a practicing Stoic, he could not resist the emotion that was welling up inside of him. For the first time in many years he took his lovely daughter in his arms and kissed her tenderly.

VII.

Junia was excited about her upcoming marriage with Quintus, but more than anything else, she kept thinking about Jesus and Christianity. He was the one upon whom Marcia had modeled her life. And as Scintilla explained more things about Christ and his teachings, she felt her heart more and more inflamed . . . as if she were falling in love with him.

"Do we know where he was born?" she asked her instructor one day.

"In a small village near Jerusalem, called Bethlehem. He was born in a stable, since there was no room for him in the inn."

Junia stared back at Scintilla almost indignantly.

"I can't understand that. If God is all-powerful, as you have taught me, how could he allow his son to be born in such a place? That is unworthy of him and of his great mission to the earth!"

Scintilla smiled slightly and got up from the chair for a moment. Then she began to laugh softly, as if to tease her young pupil.

"It's a mystery. God did not want to come to the earth in a spectacular way, but in a humble and obscure way. I think that above all it was to show us that material things don't really matter—not money or fine houses or pleasures."

The Roman girl looked to the floor self-consciously. She realized that the older woman from Gaul was describing her life perfectly. Though her father had taught her temperance and restraint, she felt a great attachment to all the fine things that she had. But she also remembered that night with the family and the apples as she was returning from the catacomb. She knew there was a great lesson for her in that event. But now it seemed to annoy her, as if the whole thing were too much for her.

"But where does that leave me, Scintilla?" she asked anxiously. "How can I love God and others, with my lifestyle? Did Jesus come only to save the poor?"

Scintilla walked to her and placed her hand on the young woman's shoulder.

"Don't worry, dear Junia. Marcia learned to find him even in the midst of a wealthy family, and so have many others. But you do have to become poor to discover him and to learn how to serve others around you."

"But how can I do all those things?" Junia asked her vehemently.

"I don't know, Miss," the slave woman answered simply. "Just pray and you'll find a way. There was a rich, young man that Jesus once asked to follow him, but he wouldn't, because he had too many things he would have to leave behind."

"I don't think that I could ever give up all my things," Junia answered frankly. "My heart is not big enough; I'm too selfish."

"If you truly loved him, you could," the older woman answered her with absolute seriousness.

The Roman girl looked quite surprised for a moment and then smiled. It was as if someone had opened the window for her in a dark and hot room.

"Scintilla," she said suddenly, "you never married, did you?"

"No, Miss."

"I think I know why. Is it the 'pearl of great price' that you spoke to me about a couple of weeks ago . . . and that *he* spoke about?"

Scintilla looked away from her shyly, as if she were a girl of twelve first hearing about love. She said nothing at first, but only nodded her head slightly. "It's the hundredfold," she said softly, and Junia knew what she meant.

VIII.

The next morning Junia walked to the atrium of her house and the garden pool that she liked so much, next to the poplar tree. The conversation she had with Scintilla on the previous day kept repeating itself in her mind: the pearl of great price, the hundredfold, to dedicate one's life as a virgin. The idea frightened yet fascinated her. She thought of the six vestal virgins who guarded the sacred flame in the sanctuary of the old forum and the immense privileges and honors that they had as part of the old Roman religion. But Scintilla was a Christian and was doing something else, for no visible reward at all. What faith it would take to do such a thing . . . to make such a total gift to God! Even if she were to become a Christian, she didn't feel that she would ever have enough strength inside of her to make such a commitment, or to persevere in it.

And yet, she reflected uneasily, Marcia did it. . . . Scintilla was doing it. Why couldn't she?

But first she had to think about Christianity itself. If she would become one of them, it would be a tremendous risk to her personally—and also to her family. She could face death, and her family the worst disgrace. She would lose all of her friends. And yet, she reflected once again, Marcia and her father had taken that tremendous risk, Scintilla had taken it, that wonderful little family in the fish cart—whom she thought about often for some reason—they had taken it.

It was insane, it was madness to decide so soon. She had just been hearing about Marcia's religion for a few months, and yet she had to admit to herself that she had accepted and loved everything about it right from the beginning. From that first evening, at Marcia's tomb, she had desired it, she wanted to know all about it.

There were so many mysteries, so many more things that she needed to know, but this did not seem to bother her. Scintilla's simple and sincere explanations had produced a deep resonance in her mind and heart. She had also begun to read some of Justin's writings on her own, and she could see the clarity and logic of his defense of Christianity. Some things she would discover later, she was sure, and some things she might never know . . . but that didn't really matter to her, to her who was such an intellectual! She was convinced that she had found a great Truth, and that was enough for her.

But if she were to become a Christian, what about Quintus? She would surely lose him too. She certainly felt attracted to him; he was noble and dependable, very good looking, and she did not doubt the sincerity of his love for her. She was sure that he would be faithful to her also, unlike many other Roman soldiers who were unfaithful to their wives. And yet, despite all of his good qualities and her attraction to him, she felt something stronger now working inside of her than her love for Quintus. It was something very good and very powerful, but she could not give it a name.

One thing she knew. She had loved Marcia more than any person she had ever known. She and her father had been a tremendous example for her. And yet now, even more than Marcia herself, she found herself wanting something else: she wanted what Marcia *had*. She so much wanted her joy and her carefree spirit. She wanted that wonderful thing, whatever it was, that had made her so cheerful and strong, that made her such a good friend. How did she get that power in her?

She remembered one of Scintilla's recent lessons about what the Christians called the Eucharist—from the Greek word meaning thanks—which was the center of their life and faith. It's what Cynthia and she had laughed about before, what seemed so preposterous and gross to them, and yet Marcia would have received it many times. Imagine, she thought to herself, if the Christians were right: imagine what it would be like for a woman to receive the body and blood of Jesus himself, who was both God and man. Imagine what it would mean for all that infinite and tender love to come into her body and her spirit, if she truly believed in him. Could this explain Marcia's unexplainable joy? Without knowing why she suddenly felt a deep thrill inside of her, and her heart was beating faster. She would really love to receive him, she would love to receive his divine life inside of her, she would really love to give herself completely, she . . .

But no, she forced herself to say no! She had to control herself and calm down. She had to use her mind and get control of her emotions, as her father was always telling her. It's obvious that to become a Christian would be a tremendous mistake, and she would lose everything. Her parents would never approve; they would be horrified. Her father might even disown her. And what if all that she had seen and felt these past months was only a game, just an illusion? Could it be that she was simply infatuated with the memory of a friend, like her father and Marcus had said? Could it be that Christianity is only a superstition, that Jesus didn't really rise from the dead, that the whole thing she had heard from Scintilla was only an ideal that no person could ever accomplish?

Agonizingly, Junia looked upward and put her hand to her head. She couldn't think anymore. She needed to escape from these troubling thoughts; she needed to get away somehow. "Jesus Christ, if you truly exist, please enlighten me . . . ," she found herself praying out loud. She walked around the courtyard a few times to relax, letting the crisp fresh breeze meet her face and trying not to think of anything. Then she walked back to the garden pool and looked at her image in the water. The overhead sun was shining brightly. She could see the outline of her face dancing on the transparent surface of the water, as she had seen it many times before: the dark hair, the curls around the forehead, the blue eyes all looked back up at her. The rays of sunshine sparkled on the tiny ripples of water, stirred up by the breeze, producing what appeared to be a ring of bright diamonds gently surrounding the reflection of her face. "A daughter of God!" she whispered to herself, and then smiled. She had decided.

IX.

As the weeks went by, Cynthia noticed little changes in her mistress. She generally seemed more cheerful than she could remember. At first Cynthia thought that it was due to her father's good fortune, but on closer examination, Junia's joyfulness seemed to be deeper.

She also felt a certain jealousy for Scintilla, since she came to see her mistress so often. It hurt her that she was not invited to those private classes, because she had always been, in a certain sense, Junia's confidante.

As far as Cynthia knew, or anybody else knew, Junia was studying Gallic culture from an educated slave woman. And

Junia would often surprise her and the family by using Gallic words at dinner; once she went into a long explanation about Gallic wedding customs, which had everyone, especially her father, extremely amused. She was becoming, Cynthia noticed, less impulsive in her commands. Before, she would clap her hands, expect immediate attention, and demand things in harsh tones. Now she seemed to be making an effort to speak more gently and, at times, would even say things like "Could you do this?" or "Would you mind doing this?" Once when she had become angry with one of the kitchen slaves over some small detail of decoration, Cynthia overheard her say afterward that she was sorry. Cynthia never heard of any aristocrats of Rome saying that to a mere servant.

What most surprised Cynthia was the way that Junia was beginning to do small favors for people, even the servants. It was something she had never seen before. One day, when Cynthia entered Junia's chamber to arrange her hair, she found all the instruments, including the combs and perfume, neatly placed on the table. In the past Cynthia had always gathered these materials while Junia sat and read. "Please, Miss," Cynthia said respectfully, "you need not do this."

"Do you mean the table and the combs?" Junia answered as she waved her slim hand absently, as if to take away importance from the matter. "Some Gallic elf did that."

The Greek servant could not convince her to avoid these menial tasks, and every morning she found all the materials neatly arranged for her when she entered her mistress's chamber.

But the most surprising event concerned a certain necklace.

Cynthia often brought costly jewels and necklaces for Junia to wear in her various social engagements, but she would rarely use them. There was one silver necklace with light blue pearls that Cynthia felt would blend marvellously with Junia's blue eyes and smooth dark hair. She tried repeatedly to have Junia wear it, but she refused each time.

One week Cynthia became ill and was confined to her room in the servant's quarters of Senator Gaius's mansion. Like most slaves in Rome, her room was little more than a stone cell with a bed. There was a small hard chair in the corner. Junia made sure that she was very well attended and asked that her own physician take care of her. Her father was disconcerted by that, but in the end he allowed it at his daughter's insistent pleading.

On the second day of her illness, the Greek girl heard some quick footsteps and excited whispering outside of her room. She sat up anxiously in bed and looked toward the entrance. To her amazement it was Junia herself, with a bouquet of flowers in her arms. Furthermore she was wearing the silver necklace with the blue pearls and her most beautiful palla.* Cynthia didn't know what to say; it was as if her mistress were visiting an empress, not a slave girl. Junia walked to her bed and kissed her on the forehead. Then she sat down graciously on the hard chair and, after some encouraging words to her, began to read her a poem.

It was a poem about the slave's birthplace, a small village near Athens. It contained many facts about the people there, and the countryside, and different stories that she had heard as a small girl growing up there. There were even some special expressions, in Greek, that only people from her town used . . . and a lullaby that her mother used to sing to her.

"All this," Cynthia was thinking to herself, "she has done for me. Why? She had to spend a long time gathering all this material."

Cynthia looked up for a long while at Junia and listened to her soft and clear voice. For a minute she seemed like a goddess to her.

---

* A cape, worn around the shoulders.

X.

Junia's only real enemies in Rome were other wealthy girls who were of marriageable age. Of them all, Livia despised her the most. She envied her for her beauty, which seemed to be so natural and which Junia seemed to take so much for granted . . . to the point of not really caring. But it was not only her physical charms; it was her intelligence as well. At banquets and parties Junia always managed to become the center of attention, not only for her elegance, but for her wit and education. At one banquet Livia felt so enraged with jealousy that she had to leave.

Whenever she could she tried to blacken Junia's name or bring up embarrassing facts about her family: "Everybody knows that Aurelia does not have a brain in her head"; "As for Marcus, he's too much in the clouds to be useful to anybody."

More than anything she envied Junia for her long line of suitors, especially for Quintus. Livia had met him at a play and had instantly liked him. But Quintus had not returned her interest. While he was impressed with Livia's mobility in Rome (she seemed to know everything about everybody) and with her cosmopolitan air, he could not stop thinking about the daughter of Gaius.

Livia detected that, which simply added to her bitterness.

"Mother, I hate her," Livia told Agrippina one day, after a party in which Junia had been especially applauded for an artistic rendering of Homer. Agrippina took her daughter's hand and rubbed it gently.

"Yes, and your father does not like Senator Gaius very much either. He has opposed him on a number of issues recently. But there's nothing we can do. Gaius will be named consul for sure, and with that his family will be the most honored family in Rome, save only the Emperor's."

Livia squirmed away from her; she could not take her mind off Junia.

"I don't think that she's so lily pure as she makes herself out to be. I wouldn't be surprised if she meets someone at night, or someone comes to see her secretly . . . like a lover."

Agrippina rose from her chair and walked slowly around the room. Suddenly she tapped one of the silver rings on her finger.

"You've just given me an idea, Daughter."

"What is it?"

"You'll see."

XI.

Scintilla was praying very hard that week. During the previous months, she had noted with great satisfaction how her pupil was progressing. Junia not only grasped things quickly, but she was also trying to integrate them into her life as faithfully as possible. Recently she had begun to pray every day on her own, using the teachings of Jesus and the apostles as a basis for her meditation. She would also tell Scintilla of the troubles she had with her emotions at times, or feelings of impatience and anger . . . and she would always listen carefully to Scintilla's advice, as if she were an older sister, and would try to follow it.

Marcia's former servant thought it was time to come to a decision. She wanted to respect the Roman girl's freedom to the maximum, but at the same time she desired with all her heart that she would say yes to the faith. After consulting with one of the priests in the city, Scintilla resolved that in her next visit she would ask Junia if she wanted to be baptized.

After the class was finished, with some hesitancy in her voice, she brought up the subject.

"Junia, we've been speaking for some time now. I've been praying about something quite important that I would like to speak to you about. We can always discuss it further if you want, but I thought . . ."

Junia needed no further introduction. She had been anxiously awaiting for her teacher to bring up the question, ever since her prayer in the atrium next to the poplar tree. She had felt unworthy to bring it up herself. Immediately she ran up to Scintilla and embraced her.

"Oh, Scintilla, you needn't be so cautious with me! Don't say anything else. It's been my deepest desire since we began to speak."

Scintilla nodded in silence, though she could not hide her joy.

"The answer is yes, Scintilla, yes!" she repeated emphatically. "With all my heart I want to be baptized. I still feel unworthy. But I'm so happy since I've learned about The Way that you can't imagine how much I've wanted it."

Junia's face was radiant. She could not stop expressing her joy, though it meant doing something unusual. She began to dance in the middle of the room with a lively Corinthian step that Marcia had once taught her. Then she crossed her arms over her breasts and looked upward saying out loud: "O God, Father of Jesus our Savior, thank you. With all my soul I want to be baptized. I want to give my whole life to you, and to serve you and others every day of it, like Marcia did."

Scintilla was overwhelmed by Junia's answer. She had no idea how deeply, and how quickly, the Redeemer's grace had penetrated the heart of her young student. But the priest had asked her to bring up something very difficult with the aristocratic Roman girl. She walked toward Junia slowly and placed her hand on her shoulder.

"I am very happy about your decision, Junia, but I have to remind you about two very important matters."

The Gallic woman's face seemed very serious all of a sudden, and Junia for a moment began to fear that she would not be allowed to be baptized after all.

"Remember, first of all, that it's very dangerous to be a Christian. If someone accuses you of it, and you refuse to deny your faith or make an offering to the Emperor's statue, you could be executed."

"I know that, but it doesn't matter," Junia said firmly, without any hesitation in her voice. She had obviously been thinking about it a lot. "What is the second thing?"

Scintilla looked at her young student carefully. She was smiling calmly, almost cheerfully, despite the fearful thing that she just had to ask of her. Then slowly, Scintilla continued.

"The second thing may be much more difficult for you. Don't forget, you're in a very high position in Rome. You are the daughter of a Roman senator, who will probably become the next consul. If you become a Christian, and if you are discovered, your family could be affected. Your father could lose his consulship, and your mother and brother disgraced."

After hearing that, Junia's expression changed. She had lost her eager smile, and her cheeks became pale. She looked down at her feet but answered calmly.

"I know that too. I've thought about it many times. Yet I still want to be a Christian. With all my strength I have prayed that our Lord would give me the grace to be a good disciple of his. And I've also asked him to protect my family, no matter what happens to me. I'm confident that he has heard my prayer."

Scintilla walked up to her and, without saying a word, knelt down in front of her. Junia tried to stop her and cried out impulsively, "No, Scintilla, what are you doing? What are you doing? No!"

"Please, dearest Junia," the old woman had tears in her eyes. "Let me do this for you." Then she took Junia's lovely hands into her own and kissed them. "Be thankful, child, for the things that his grace is doing for you. You are speaking like the bravest among us, already."

XII.

Culebros had been watching the Senator's mansion for over two weeks. He had entered with a multitude of Gaius's assistants on two occasions and had a chance to see Junia one of the times. He had also seen her several times before, since he was one of Agrippina's personal slaves and had served at several of her banquets.

All of Junia's activities had been very normal for the previous two weeks, but Culebros was rather curious about the frequent visits of an elderly plebeian lady to the Senator's house. One day he had seen Junia escort her to the door where the two spoke for a while very earnestly. Culebros followed Scintilla to her home that evening, a small flat in one of the poorer tenements. Shortly Scintilla left the flat and began to walk quickly among the crowds. Agrippina's spy followed her, and much to his surprise, she walked to the outskirts of the city, toward the old Jewish cemeteries—and the Christian catacombs. Following at some distance, he noticed that Scintilla joined a group of men and women, and together they entered one of the catacombs.

At first he thought of mentioning this fact to his mistress, but he knew that many Christian slaves worked during the day and occasionally went to the catacombs at night to pray for their dead. He preferred to wait and keep observing.

One night, just after the sun set, Culebros noticed a hooded figure leave one of the side entrances of the Senator's mansion. He couldn't tell whether it was a man or a woman, but it seemed rather slim to be a man. Maybe one of Gaius's adolescent servants, he thought to himself.

Without giving it too much importance, he followed the person for a while. At a certain corner of the city, a fish cart stopped and the mysterious figure climbed aboard. He could hear laughter and excited voices: a man, a woman, a boy, and a girl were greeting the new arrival. Within a minute the cart was in motion, heading toward the outskirts of Rome. Culebros, on horseback, followed them carefully, at a distance.

For Junia it was the happiest night of her life. She joked with the driver of the cart about that night, several months before, when they had gathered apples on the road together. Since then, Scintilla had told her that she could trust them absolutely and that they would be happy to attend her baptism. Junia had arranged to meet them at a certain corner and travel to the catacombs together. It was decided that she would be baptized there privately, outside of the Easter vigil, and outside of the city, where it would not attract attention. She had learned the names of the family from Scintilla: the father was Justus, the mother Constantia, the boy Timothaeus, and the girl Carmina.

"You thought I was a Christian that first night, didn't you?" Junia teased the twelve-year-old boy who sat next to her. "Well, now I'm going to become one truly, and I'm very happy to have you all with me."

"We've been praying to the Mother of Jesus for you, Miss," the boy answered, and Junia hugged him appreciatively.

As they approached the catacomb entrance, she could feel her heart beating very fast. For an instant she was afraid and even wanted to go back. It was a new life, and a new adventure that she was embarking on, and she realized that after tonight her life would never be the same. She had thought about it many times before and doubted her strength to be a really good Christian. But then Scintilla taught her a verse from one of the Psalms: "The Lord is my shepherd; I shall not fear." And she would imagine that she was a sheep nestled on Jesus' strong shoulders and that he was speaking to her, telling her how much he loved her. Junia said that psalm silently as they approached the catacomb entrance.

Scintilla greeted them at the entrance, and once inside the cave, Junia drew back her veil. The light from the torches reflected her fine features and bright eyes. The little girl looked up at her in amazement. "Miss, how pretty you are!" she could not help saying out loud. Junia bent over and patted her forehead. "Now, with God's grace, I hope to become truly beautiful. Please pray for me."

Junia wanted to visit Marcia's tomb once more before the ceremony. She knelt before it and placed her hand on the inscription. "Marcia," she whispered, "soon I'll really be your sister. Thank you for remembering me from heaven, and please help me to be strong now." She rose slowly and moved a few steps to her right, to the fresco of the Good Shepherd. She looked up at the youthful face, at the smiling eyes, at the strong shoulders . . . and a prayer rose within her. She was thrilled to think that in just a few minutes the divine life of Jesus would be dwelling in her soul, cleansing her from all her sins, and sharing with her the greatest of gifts: his infinite love.

Because of Junia's high position in Rome, and because of the danger of recognition, there were very few people at her baptism: the priest, Scintilla, and the family. She felt very unworthy to receive such a gift, and as the water was poured over her and she could hear the priest saying, "I baptize you in the name of the Father, and of the Son, and of the Holy Spirit," her heart was filled with a joy that she could not describe. Scintilla heard her say, over and over again during the ceremony, "Thank you, Lord Jesus, thank you, thank you."

Immediately afterward, when she had answered certain questions about the faith that were put to her by the priest, she received the sacrament of Confirmation and the Sacred Eucharist. After singing a hymn that she had practiced with Scintilla, she spent a long time on her knees, in silence, clothed with the white robe given to those who had just received Baptism. Her teacher was afraid that she would catch a cold since she remained kneeling so long on the damp clay. But Junia didn't mind the dampness or the cold.

It was impossible for her to express to Jesus all the love and gratitude that she was feeling at that moment.

When she finally rose from the ground, her face was radiant. She looked at those around her and wanted to kiss everybody, including the priest and the guard. The women immediately gathered around her and embraced her: Scintilla first, then Constantia, then little Carmina. Scintilla, of the three, was the only one crying. Junia caressed the little girl and kissed her on the forehead and on both cheeks. "Will you keep praying to the Virgin Mary for me?" she asked her softly. "Don't worry, Miss Junia, the entire family is praying for you," answered a deep masculine voice from behind her. It was the little girl's father.

Little by little the very joyful group moved toward the exit of the catacomb. With great hesitation and regret, Junia left her white baptismal robe in the catacomb. It was very hard for her to do, since it meant so much to her. As they left the cave she kept her veil off, thinking that there could be no danger of recognition in that place, and at that time. Happily she climbed into the family's humble cart once again, in the back, as she had done the first night.

After the fish cart had left, and the guard had reentered the cave, Culebros slowly eased himself to the ground. He had been able to see the entire group from a tree that he had climbed; above all, he had taken careful note of Junia. He would have an interesting story to tell to Agrippina and Livia, and he hoped to be rewarded handsomely. But he would wait a while, to see if she came back again.

XIII.

Junia couldn't sleep that night. Many thoughts kept racing through her mind. She was thinking of how selfish she would be to keep the Lord Jesus, with all his truth and love, only for herself. She wanted to reach out to everyone, to have everyone know Christ and his message; it would make them so happy, as happy as she was in that moment.

First of all, she thought of her family. There was her father; he would be the hardest of all, since he was convinced that Christianity was an enemy of the Roman state and filled with criminals. "Father, if you only knew!" she whispered to herself. "Christianity is the only real friend that Rome has." Then there was Marcus, so intellectual . . . *too* intellectual. How could she ever convince him that there was only one God, and even more, that he knows and cares for each human being? How could she ever explain to him that Jesus rose from the dead? He would laugh at her and think that she had been duped by somebody. And then there was her mother. Junia felt sorry because she had often scorned and rejected her mother; she was so simple and loyal really, but caught up with the fashions of the world. Would she be able to understand where the real treasures of life could be found?

Junia shook her head slowly at the task before her. She would need a lot of help. She made the sign of the cross, from her forehead, to her lips, to her breast, to her shoulders, and then made an act of faith in God and his providence. Finally she fell asleep.

Shortly after dawn she was awakened by the sound of the assistants greeting her father in the atrium. "*Ave Gaie. Salve, Illustrissime!*" they were shouting, trying to get his attention. At first she felt annoyed at them, as she had on other occasions, but she forced herself to remember that she was a Christian now. A Christian had to foster within himself the same sentiments that the Master had. And she realized that at that moment her sentiments were not of love but of anger. She decided, as if it were a game, to play a trick on herself, as a kind of penance for her lack of love.

Quickly she put on her tunic and quietly left her chamber. She slipped around the corner and looked toward the atrium, where her father was receiving all those men with the shabby looking togas. "Yes," she thought to herself, "they're all shabby looking; they're pushing each other; they're swearing. But Jesus died for each of them. The least I can do is to pray for them." And then, beginning with Bombolinus, who was always in the front row, she looked at each one—short and tall, with beards and without—and prayed that each would some day know the Master as she had. Finally she prayed for her father, who had his back to her. It was the longest prayer of all. As she returned to bed, she kept saying, "Lord, may I never think of me but only of thee." She made a little rhyme of it, until she fell asleep again.

Cynthia was concerned about her mistress, since she hadn't awakened early that morning. Many times she was up even before the *clientes* arrived. Cynthia tiptoed to her chamber and knocked lightly on the door. She heard a stirring, then a soft voice: "Who is it?"

"It's Cynthia, Miss Junia. Is everything all right?"

"Oh, very much all right," Junia's cheerful voice answered back. "Please come in for a while."

Cynthia entered and found Junia propped up on her cushion with a lively, almost mischievous, smile on her face.

"Cynthia, Cynthia," the Roman girl lifted her voice as if she were singing, "I have never felt so wonderful."

"I'm glad, Miss," Cynthia answered, though she looked down when she said it. There was a note of despondency in her voice.

"And you, Cynthia, how do you feel?"

Cynthia smiled appreciatively. A year ago her mistress would have never asked that question, but now it seemed natural to her and to both of them.

"Oh, Miss, my father is very sick, and they aren't treating him well at all. I know that I am just a slave, and so is he, but unless I can do something I'm afraid that he'll grow worse."

"Don't say that you're just a slave," Junia raised her voice unexpectedly, as if she were angry at something.

"Pardon, Miss?"

"Never mind. Where does your father live?"

"He's a livery servant at Balbo's mansion."

"Balbo? He has a very bad reputation for treating slaves. You should have told me earlier."

"I would have, Miss, but I didn't think that you could do anything for him."

Junia rose quickly from bed. She was interiorly giving thanks to the Good Shepherd for this chance to serve somebody else, on her very first day as his disciple. She had not expected it but quickly began to put on her travelling tunic and hood.

"Miss, where are you going?"

"You mean, where are *we* going? We're going to visit your father and talk to Balbo."

It did not take long for the two young women to reach Balbo's mansion. The ex-consul, famous for his gruffness, was amazed to see the beautiful daughter of Gaius at his door. Junia nodded to him politely and offered him her hand.

"I am honored to have you, Miss," he said, rather uncharacteristically. He was caught so off guard by the visit that he did not know what to say.

"This is Cynthia, Sir Balbo," Junia motioned delicately to her servant. "I understand that her father is sick; he is one of your livery slaves."

Balbo glanced absently at Cynthia. It was not his custom to talk to slaves, except to give orders. Junia went on, "We would like to visit him, if you don't mind. His name is Philos."

Balbo began to regain his composure, getting over his initial surprise. He felt annoyed at the whole idea and couldn't understand Junia's intentions.

"Philos? That old buzzard? Why would such a pretty thing like you want to visit him?" Balbo asked sarcastically, almost aggressively.

Junia felt suddenly embarrassed. Blood was racing to her cheeks as she realized that she had come on an impulse and that it must seem strange to everybody, including Cynthia, that a young woman of such high rank would visit a common slave. It could even occasion some gossip, which Rome was very prone to repeat, being a city of constant rumors. With a quick silent prayer she asked her Lord for help.

"Because he's human, Sir Balbo, he's human," Junia said softly.

The tough old Roman looked at her with complete bewilderment, trying to strain his ears to understand her.

"He's human," Junia repeated more forcefully. "He's human and he can suffer and feel pain like you and me. That's why I want to visit him. Can you understand that?"

Balbo gasped for a moment and shook his head.

"You women are crazy. Go ahead then. It means nothing to me. I always took you for a bright girl, Junia."

Then he called one of his slaves who accompanied the two young women to Philos's room.

As Cynthia predicted, the cubicle was filthy. There was excrement on the floor and on the bed, and the air was reeking. Cynthia did not want her mistress to enter, but Junia insisted. Together the two girls cleaned the room, using some rags and containers that they had brought with them; they also washed the old man and changed his bed linen. Since the room had no window, it was impossible to ventilate it.

"We've got to find some solution for this," Junia said. "The best thing would be to move your father to our house, but that will be very hard since he's Balbo's slave. Don't worry, Cynthia, we'll find a way."

As they were carried in the litter back to the Senator's mansion, Cynthia noticed that her mistress kept looking frequently out of the window, at the crowds surging around them. She seemed very intent on something, and her lips were moving slowly.

"Miss, are you looking for someone?"

Junia turned to her eagerly, as if she had just discovered something great.

"Cynthia, do you see all those people out there? Fat and thin, tall and short, white and black? Do you know that each one of them is really very loveable?"

Cynthia looked at her incredulously.

"Pardon, Miss, but you must be joking. How can they all be loveable? I'm sure that many of them are downright scoundrels."

Junia narrowed her eyes a bit and looked sideways at her servant. "I know of someone who died with two scoundrels—one on his right and one on his left—and he loved them both."

Then she laughed suddenly and gave Cynthia a playful shove. The Greek girl could not understand the very unusual mood that her mistress was in that day.

XIV.

In her first week as a Christian Junia forced herself to do two things: to pray frequently and to find ways of helping those around her. She did not want to be applauded or recognized for what she did, since she understood that to pass unnoticed would be the purest imitation of Jesus' life, and that of his closest apostles.

Above all, she prayed for her family. After Marcia and Scintilla, they were the people to whom she felt the closest in her life. She kept thinking of ways to help them understand Christianity and to bring up the subject with them. Unfortunately her father and mother were very busy, with invitations for dinner almost every afternoon. One morning she saw her brother studying a scroll in the courtyard just after he returned from Strabo's Institute. As usual he was perspiring profusely, since he had just returned from the hot and crowded streets of Rome. Junia loved to tease him about that, but this time she wanted to do it in a special way.

She took off her sandals and very quietly walked up behind him. Before he could turn around she had her arms
around him, and was kissing him on the back of the neck.

"Junia, please," Marcus said irritably. "I was reading."

His sister drawled back, "You shouldn't complain. Not too
many girls would want to hug you the way you are now.
Ugh! You're sweating like a horse!"

And at that she began to wipe off some of the perspira-
tion from his forehead with her long dark hair.

Marcus couldn't help smiling and uttered something like
"thank you" then continued to read. But Junia was determined to keep his attention.

"The theory of the many gods is pretty outdated nowa-
days, isn't that so, Marcus?" she began nonchalantly.

"One might say so," Marcus said absently as he continued
to read.

"Well, I believe in the theory of the one God."

Her brother put down his scroll and looked at her with
some interest. "Is that so? And how do you define this one
God?"

"Oh, Marcus, you're always defining things! Let's just say
that I define him as someone who loves me very much," and
then she added, "and you too."

"That's strange. A God who loves us. It really couldn't be
the Stoic god or the Pythagorean principle, could it?"

"No, not at all," she answered with mounting fervor in
her voice. "My God is a very special one who knows and
cares about every human being, even the smallest and the
poorest."

It seemed to Marcus that his sister was almost romanti-
cizing, as if dreaming about a great, handsome hero. He
laughed out loud; it was his turn to tease her.

"You seem to be talking about a lover, more than a god.
Tell me, dear sister, do you love your God more than
Quintus?"

Junia looked at him seriously for a moment; she had only

thought about that once before. She was hurt by Marcus's light-handed teasing, but she tried to control herself. She nodded slowly and simply said, "Yes."

"I can't believe it! You love something you don't see more than a man whom you can see and touch! You must introduce me to this wonderful God of yours."

"I would be glad to do that, but I'm afraid that you would reject him."

"Why don't you tell me about it, Junia? You know that I have an open mind; you remember that at one time I was even considering the Christian religion."

"And what made you stop?" She could feel her heart beating faster as she asked.

"Quite frankly, I couldn't accept the fact that God could become a human being."

Junia recalled a passage from one of the letters of Paul that Scintilla had given her.

"But Marcus, if God is all-powerful, why couldn't he become a man? The one who made all things should certainly have power over what he made."

Marcus reflected for a moment. He had always respected his sister's good mind; it seemed to him that she was using words and ideas in a way he hadn't heard before.

"Junia, it would be degrading for a deathless god to become a mere mortal. He would not be a god then."

Junia laughed delightedly at that and clapped her hands, as if it were all a game.

"But Marcus, that's the whole point, don't you see? The Christians believe that God became man without ceasing to be God. Jesus Christ was both God and man."

Marcus stared at her.

"Junia, it's too much to believe. Why would an unlimited and independent being want to become limited and dependent? Why would he allow himself to be crucified?"

Junia didn't answer at first. She went up to her brother and sat beside him; gently she took his hand into hers.

"Why would he allow himself to be crucified? Because, as I said before, this God happens to love us. He became a baby and died for us . . . because he loved us."

Marcus looked into his sister's bright blue eyes. He had never heard her talk about anything before with such conviction. He really didn't know what to say and simply looked down at his scroll again. "I'll think about it," he said weakly and continued to read.

THE PAIN OF HIS CROSS

I.

The next time she saw Scintilla, Junia told her how happy she was to be a Christian but that she found it hard to live as Jesus wanted and to be cheerful all the time. Many times she felt moody and angry about things. Scintilla told her not to give up trying and that God's grace would help her. She found it even harder to bring her parents and brother closer to Christ's teaching. Scintilla told her not to worry and that the most important thing was to pray for them and give them good example. God in his infinite wisdom would choose the right time and the right hour. Besides praying for them each day, the Roman girl decided to offer two sacrifices each day for them: not to take Cyprian dates, which she liked so much; and to sit on a hard bench when she read in the morning.

With Cynthia, she resolved to speak more directly. Junia felt that she had a good enough rapport with her servant to bring up the topic of Christianity, though she was not sure how far she would get. She did know that Cynthia was a refined and loyal girl, and she began to pray for her from that moment.

That evening, after Scintilla had left, Junia received word that her father wanted to see her in his study. Junia was happy for the chance to see him, but when she entered, it was obvious that he was quite worried about something. He was bent over a small piece of papyrus on the table and was nervously tapping his fingers. The young woman was surprised because her father was always very calm and reasonable in his reactions to things. Perhaps he needed comforting; she felt very ready to give it, more than ever before.

"Father, you called for me?" she asked with an affectionate smile.

The Senator did not look up. He handed his daughter the recently opened papyrus, and with a hoarse voice, as if trying to hold back his anger, he asked her to read it.

Junia took it and read the following message:

GAIUS: I HAVE EYEWITNESS PROOF THAT YOUR DAUGHTER IS A CHRISTIAN; SHE WAS SEEN IN THE CATACOMBS WITH OTHER CHRISTIANS JUST ONE MONTH AGO. MY SILENCE IN THIS MATTER MUST BE BOUGHT, MY FRIEND. COME AND SEE ME TOMORROW, AND I WILL TELL YOU WHAT YOU MUST DO.

ANTONIUS

It was like a lightening bolt for Junia. She was speechless and unable to react. Her father stood up from the table slowly, as if trying to master himself.

"I know, of course, that this isn't true and only an empty charge directed at me for political reasons. Antonius wants to ruin me; he always has. Nevertheless I wanted to show this to you, so you could tell me how absurd it is."

Junia looked away suddenly from her father; she felt very helpless and confused, as if a huge storm were about to descend on her. She didn't expect that God would put her to the test so soon after becoming a Christian. For the moment, she preferred to evade the issue.

"Being in the catacombs doesn't make one a Christian . . ." she said weakly.

"What does that mean?" her father asked her with a disturbed voice. "Does that mean that you really *were* in the catacombs?"

Junia looked away again. She wasn't ready for this; it was too much for her.

Senator Gaius, making a great effort, tried to keep his voice steady.

"Tell me, Daughter, were you in the catacombs one month ago?"

When she was nine years old, Junia remembered that she had lied once to her father in order to avoid a punishment. She had always regretted that, and she would not lie now.

"Yes," she answered. She could feel her whole body trembling as she spoke.

Gaius clenched his fist and looked away from her in disgust. "Stupid, stupid," he was muttering to himself.

"How could you do such a thing?" he asked her bitterly.

Junia moved toward him, as if to throw herself into his arms. She desperately wanted him to understand the wonderful thing she had discovered, though she felt totally helpless.

"No, Junia," her father said, as if suddenly repulsed by her. "Go to your room. I must think. Go to your room. There has to be a way out of this."

Junia tried to move toward him again as she tried to hold back her tears.

"Go to your room, Junia," he said with a sudden calm, but with a coldness that she had never heard before.

II.

"Good Shepherd, help me. Good Shepherd, embrace your lost sheep." As she ran to her chamber, Junia kept repeating these prayers almost impulsively. She felt very confused and betrayed, as if someone had just stabbed her in the back. Who could have seen her that day in the catacombs? Only Scintilla, the family, the priest, and the guard. Which one of them had betrayed her, and why?

She groped for an answer. How could Jesus, who was so good, permit such a thing to happen? Was he not the savior of the world, in whom she had believed so much? One of those she had trusted, one of those who had brought her to the faith, had apparently betrayed her. Could it have been Scintilla herself? The thought horrified her. For the first time Junia could feel her faith being shaken; perhaps her new religion was not worth so much pain. . . .

"No!" she cried out loud, shaking her head and trying to reject the thought.

She remembered that Jesus was betrayed, also. It would be pride for her to expect better treatment. Rather, she thought to herself, she should be happy because Jesus had chosen to let her share in his suffering more closely, and so soon after she was cleansed in Baptism. Hadn't Scintilla warned her about the danger of persecution before she became a Christian; but what if—the haunting thought returned to her— what if it was Scintilla herself who had betrayed her?

Once in her room she knelt down and prayed out loud: "O Lord Jesus Christ, I trust in you. I'll never abandon you, who are my only true love. Even if it was my teacher who betrayed me, I'll never betray you. Please help me to be strong."

She made the sign of the cross and rose slowly. She felt more confident, though she could not shake off a sense of dread that was coming over her. If the Lord helped her, she was sure that she could endure anything. "Anything?" she asked herself for the first time. . . . "Even torture?"

At that instant someone knocked at her door.

"Who's there?" Junia asked with some anxiety.

"It's Cynthia, Mistress Junia. May I come in?"

"Of course."

When Cynthia entered, she noticed immediately that her mistress had been crying. Her eyes looked red, and her hair was disheveled.

"I'm sorry, Miss; shall I return later?" she asked discreetly.

"Oh, no, Cynthia," Junia was quick to reply. She wiped away the tears and forced herself to smile. "I was feeling lonely just now. Don't mind the tearful face; it will go away.

Junia was surprised to discover how cheerful she had become, as if nothing had happened. She realized, in an instant, that her happiness was coming from God's grace—since it couldn't be coming from herself.

But Cynthia looked very serious, almost solemn.

"May we sit down, Miss? I think I could express myself better that way."

At that the two young women sat down on the Tuscan marble bench that Aurelia had recently bought for her daughter.

"I don't know where to begin," Cynthia said haltingly. "Let me just say that I'm very grateful for all that you have done for me, Miss. I have noticed the favors, the flowers you brought me, and the way you've helped my father by sending your own physician, and all the kind things that you . . ."

Junia put her forefinger to Cynthia's mouth. "Hush," she reprimanded her quietly. "You're going to make me conceited."

"But Miss," Cynthia insisted, "I have to thank you. I have to. And what's more, I want to ask you why you are doing all these things for me. Nobody else . . . no other mistress . . . has ever treated me so kindly. Please teach me to do them too, because they're wonderful and they do so much good."

Junia looked at her maidservant calmly. Little by little a smile creased her lips until it seemed to radiate over her entire face. She could feel a great contentment and gratitude welling up inside of her. She understood, in an instant, that now was the time to tell Cynthia about The Way.

"Why do I do these things? It's very simple. I'm a Christian, Cynthia, and I'm trying to live my faith with all my strength."

Cynthia's eyes opened wide for a moment, but then she smiled, as if to confirm something that she had known before.

"Does this shock you, Cynthia?" Junia asked quickly.

"No, Miss. I've actually suspected it for some time. Ever

since Marcia died, I've noticed something in you, something different. And ever since you began to speak with Scintilla. There's something about her, too, that's different. She's a Christian, too, isn't she? I can see now what the Christians mean when they say that we should love one another."

Cynthia looked directly into her mistress's eyes, unembarrassed, and continued, "You've shown me that, Miss Junia."

The Roman girl said a silent prayer; it just seemed to come to her. "*Deo omnis gloria*" (to God all the glory). She did not want to be complimented for what she had done.

"No," she replied to Cynthia. "From now on you must simply call me Junia."

Cynthia nodded in silence. Then she added, almost timidly and with great respect: "I would be very grateful if you could teach me something about Christianity."

Junia clapped her hands and laughed out loud for sheer delight. She had not expected anything like this to happen, and she was amazed at how quickly grace was working in Cynthia's soul.

"Teach you, do you say? You have chosen a very inexperienced professor. I have just learned it myself, Cynthia, and am still learning. But I will try my best."

And immediately, there in her room, she began to explain to her servant the first lesson that she had learned from Scintilla: how God was One and Almighty, and how he took a personal interest in the life of every human being, rich and poor, slave and free.

III.

After receiving Antonius's note, Gaius went to work immediately. Through different channels, he found out that Antonius's only witness was a slave named Culebros, who had seen Junia and others one night at the catacombs. He felt very relieved, because he knew that Roman law prohibited a slave from giving testimony against a Roman citizen, or the daughter of a Roman citizen. Legally Junia was safe, and Gaius prepared to defend her against further attacks.

The Senator had a long talk with Junia shortly afterward. He explained to her that the only witness that Antonius had was a slave, and that for the moment, she was free from prosecution. Though he didn't know it, this information brought great peace to his daughter—not so much because she was free from prosecution, but because now she was sure that no Christian had betrayed her. Gaius prohibited her from returning to the catacombs, or any Christian gathering place, and from seeing Scintilla again.

Though it was hard for her, Junia resigned herself to not seeing her dear friend again, or other Christians. She could not banish her memory of them, however, as her father had told her to do. She yearned for the day when she could receive the Eucharist again and speak with those of her faith. In the meantime she dedicated herself completely to the task of teaching Cynthia. They had to be very careful and choose places in the Senator's mansion where no one could hear their conversation.

For a week it seemed that Junia was out of danger. But neither she nor her father had taken into account one of Rome's chief vices: gossip. Livia and Agrippina quickly spread the news about Junia to all the important families in the city; from them word spread to the common people and the slaves, until all of Rome was talking about it: the lovely daughter of Gaius was a Christian.

Besides Culebros's report, there were plenty of circumstances that made Junia's Christianity very plausible: she had been a close friend of Marcia, who had been executed for the crime of Christianity; she had received frequent visits from an elderly Christian lady, a former servant of Marcia's household; she had been known to do unusual things, like visiting slaves who were sick.

Gaius's political enemies took full advantage of the situation and made sure that the news reached the Emperor. He was quite saddened by it, since he had great respect for Gaius and had sincerely thought that he would make a good consul. He had also heard that one of his best Praetorian Guards, Quintus, intended to marry Junia. With a heavy heart he sent a message to Gaius, marked with the imperial seal. It was very brief:

> GAIUS: THE AIR MUST BE CLEARED. I HOPE YOU REALIZE THAT NOT ONLY YOUR NAME, BUT THE EMPEROR'S, IS AT STAKE. YOUR DAUGHTER MUST TAKE THE OATH AND OFFER INCENSE TO THE IMPERIAL STATUE.
>
> CAESAR

IV.

As rumors spread about her in the city, Junia found that the number of invitations to banquets and parties *increased*. "It seems," she would joke to Cynthia, "that I've become a combination of celebrity and monster now." But her father gave her strict orders that she was not to leave the mansion.

Junia was amazed that most people were not really interested in whether she was a Christian or not; they just liked to speculate about it. In her own family nobody even dared to ask her that question; perhaps it would have been too bitter a revelation for them.

She kept praying that the whole thing would pass over, since she was firmly convinced that she could continue being a Christian and still lead a normal life in Rome. She had hoped that through her words and example she could bring Christ's message to many of her peers. In the meantime, she was delighted with Cynthia's interest in her religion and carefully prepared each lesson. Scintilla had given her a scroll of excerpts from Saint Paul's letters, which she kept carefully hidden in her chamber. She hadn't even told Cynthia about it. She would often read passages from it, not only to prepare lessons for Cynthia, but to nourish the divine life that was growing in her own soul. One passage that she particularly liked was the letter to her own countrymen: "Who shall separate us from the love of Christ? Shall tribulation, or distress, or persecution, or hunger, or nakedness, or danger, or the sword? But in all these things we overcome because of him who has loved us."

The Apostle's brave words greatly comforted the lovely Roman girl. She would read them when she felt weak or fearful about the future, which day by day seemed more uncertain for her. Though she knew that there was no binding evidence against her, it was obvious that all of Rome was talking about her and that many people suspected that she was a Christian. She continued to pray that the whole matter be forgotten, but if it weren't, she also prayed that she would be strong.

One night her father called her to his study. It was one week before the appointing of the new consuls. Junia dreaded this meeting; he had been particularly distraught the week before about something, which was completely unlike him and opposed to his Stoicism. And though he said nothing, Junia knew that she was the cause of his agony. It was like a sword piercing her mind, because she cared for her father very much. But upon entering she was surprised to see him remarkably calm. He asked her to sit down, as he rose slowly from his working table.

"Daughter, I'll be very direct. The situation has become very serious; I've received a message from the Emperor himself. He wants you to take the oath."

Junia looked at the floor. That could mean only one oath; the oath to the statue of the Emperor, accompanied by an offering of wine and incense and the public renouncing of Christ. It was the same oath that Marcia and her father had refused to take.

Her lips were trembling, but she managed to say clearly, "Father, I cannot do that; I will never do that."

Gaius looked at her with amazement, as if he had heard

an impossible statement. His daughter had never defied him before.

"You will do as you are told, Junia," he said irritably.

Junia refused to live under any more pretenses; she felt she could hide the truth no longer. "Father," she said calmly, "you never asked me if I was a Christian." Then she added gently, looking into her father's eyes, "Father, I am a Christian."

Gaius could endure it no longer. He pounded his fist on the table.

"That's enough. It's not only treason to be a Christian, it's immoral. How could you be so deceived? Did your impish friend Marcia or that old Gallic witch brainwash you?"

Junia was surprised to see how calm she had become. She was able to overlook the obvious sarcasm and penetrate to the core of his problem.

"Father, what you are saying is not so. Christianity is a religion of sacrifice and duty, even more than the Stoics teach; Marcia and Scintilla are the most generous and dutiful people I have ever known. In the end, Christianity will help the Roman Empire because it is making people better on the inside, where it counts."

Gaius saw that he could get nowhere by arguing. He looked at his uncompromising daughter and shook his head slowly. He must use his last resort. He stood erect, adjusted his toga to its full length, and spoke to her solemnly: "My daughter Junia, by the power of my authority over you, and as head of this household, I command you to take the anti-Christian oath."

The calm that Junia had felt before was now engulfed by a thousand conflicting emotions. She realized that a father's power over his household was one of the most sacred things in Rome. And even though it had been eroded by permissiveness over the past two hundred years, and even though many of her young, clever friends laughed at it, she had never laughed. She truly believed in it.

Junia clasped her hands desperately and lowered her head to her knees. She could feel her whole body trembling.

"I can't do it, Father," she said, almost inaudibly. "I can't do it." She looked up at him, as if pleading with him, as tears came to her eyes. Her lips began to tremble again.

Gaius did not notice the tears nor hear the pleading voice. He was shocked, and his face had become white with rage. He could only think of how ungrateful this daughter of his had become . . . she who had always been his favorite, in whom he had put so much hope. He raised his hand, which was shaking violently, and struck her in the face.

V.

Junia ran to her room; it was the first time that her father had ever hit her. She was sobbing violently, uncontrollably. Her father had meant so much to her, and now she felt alone and totally helpless. She knew that one of the greatest supports in her life had been taken from her, suddenly and cruelly. She couldn't understand why God was testing her so painfully, but she was more and more resolved never to leave her new-born faith, which was like a beautiful young child growing within her.

After a while there was a light knock at the door.

Aurelia had not understood much about the political implications of Christianity, and oftentimes she would appear absentminded and slow with her family. But she could be very shrewd in dealing with her children and had an affection for them that was deep and unfeigned. She was determined to save her daughter from her blindness.

"May I come in?" she asked softly.

"Yes," her daughter answered with a hoarse voice. Aurelia approached her bedside, and her daughter sat up when she entered the room. Aurelia sat on the bed and caressed her soft cheeks, wiping away the tears with her handkerchief. Then she kissed her daughter and asked her to lie down. For a long time she sat in silence, as her daughter stared at the ceiling.

"Are you calmer now?" she asked at length.

"Yes, Mother," Junia answered.

"Junia, you should try to reconsider. Your father has only your good in mind."

"Please, Mother," Junia whispered in agony, "let's not talk about it."

"Junia," her mother insisted, "you're young and intelligent and have a wonderful future before you. It would be foolish to throw all that away for some foreign religion, from a land you've never seen."

Then she stroked her daughter's soft, dark hair and kissed her again.

"What do you have in your hand, Mama?"

"A letter."

"From whom?"

"From Quintus, and addressed to you. Shall I read it?"

All the attraction that Junia had felt for the young Praetorian seemed to well up again inside of her. She reflected for a moment, then shook her head and closed her eyes.

"No, I don't want to hear it," she said decisively. "Take it away please."

"But he loves you, Junia. How can you be so hard-hearted so as not even to listen?"

"I don't want to hear, Mother," Junia repeated, this time more vehemently.

"Dear Daughter," her mother said tenderly as she caressed her face again, "you've never really known a man's embrace, have you?"

Though her daughter's eyes were closed, Aurelia could see tears streaming down her cheeks.

"Quintus loves you, Junia. He's strong, smart, and would make a wonderful husband for you—better than many in Rome. And he's flesh and blood, my dear, not some invisible spirit, or some mystical Jewish preacher crucified over a hundred years ago."

Junia sat up quickly and covered her ears with her hands. She rubbed them vigorously, as if trying to rub away the words she had just heard.

"No more, Mother, no more!" she cried out. "Please go now."

Aurelia sighed loudly, patted her daughter's hand, and left the room. She could not understand her reaction when she had spoken about the crucified Jew, but she felt confident that her words would eventually seep in and Junia would change her mind. She took Quintus's message with her and decided to use it on another occasion.

VI.

The week's events were also taking their toll on Marcus. In his own way he was quite worried about his sister. He was very annoyed by remarks that his intellectual friends kept making. "I thought your sister was intelligent; at least she always struck me that way." "How could she believe that series of fairy tales anyway?" Before such remarks Marcus always defended Junia with a few favorable ideas about Christianity . . . though he couldn't go too far, or else he would be suspected.

What he would not tolerate were slurs on his sister's reputation. Again and again, there were references to supposed immoral acts in Christian meetings. One of Junia's rejected suitors, who still felt insulted at having lost her to Quintus, even accused her publicly of having a lover on the side. Marcus was present at the time and asked him to take back what he said. When the man refused, Marcus hit him on the jaw, and this led to a bigger brawl. The incident simply added to the gossip that all of Rome was repeating about the Senator and his family.

Shortly afterward, Marcus decided to have a long talk

with his sister. His mother and father urged him to do so, each with different reasons. And Marcus had some ideas of his own that he thought might sway her.

He found Junia in her room. She had left it very rarely over the past three days and had eaten hardly anything. Her eyes were red from crying, but when he entered the room she brushed away her tears and did her best to smile.

Marcus felt a momentary repulsion toward his sister. In his opinion, and in his father's, tears came from a weak temperament. He was convinced that Junia was letting her emotions get the better of her and that she should have seen the error of Christianity long before. He also believed that she had some strong emotional attachment to her dead friend, Marcia, which she had not been able to overcome without the necessary maturity.

Marcus decided not to take any detours, he wanted to enter the matter directly, with the frankness of a brother who had spoken about deep things before with his sister.

"Junia, I can't understand you. You're bringing all of this upon yourself and us—and for some new idea that has not really been proven."

To his astonishment, instead of getting angry or crying, Junia's smile seemed to grow bigger. She looked at him playfully and said, "Marcus, dear brother, did you know that my God is older than all the Greek and Roman gods?"

"What do you mean by older?"

"Simply that he always was and always will be."

Marcus thought for a moment. He would have liked to pursue the idea of eternity for a bit, and bring up things about the Stoic and Platonic principles of the universe, but that would distract him from his main purpose—to convince her to take the anti-Christian oath.

He had an idea.

"Is this Christian god of yours all-powerful?"

"Yes."

"Then listen, dear sister. If this god of yours has always

existed, and is all-powerful, I am sure that you would not offend him by taking an oath. How could you, a mere mortal, offend such an eternal being by saying a few words?"

Junia shook her head impatiently and stamped her foot on the floor.

"But Marcus, this God can read hearts. Don't you know that the words of an oath show what is in the heart? If words don't correspond to what is in the heart, they're a lie."

Marcus put both hands on her shoulders and looked at her steadily.

"Well, Junia, that's my point! Why are you so afraid to lie about some Being so great, so far away, that couldn't care less about you?"

Junia lowered her glance for a moment. Then she lifted her eyes and looked at her brother's, almost defiantly.

"But he *does* care about me. He sent his only son to die for me."

Marcus turned away from her; he did not want to prolong the discussion any more. He felt that he was trying to move a boulder.

"Junia, here's my advice to you as a brother. Take the oath. When you have to say the words that curse Jesus Christ, say them, but in your heart bless him. Then you're not lying to yourself, and you're remaining true to your God."

Junia narrowed her eyes and looked at her brother indignantly.

"And would you do that to your best friend?"

Marcus stared at her blankly.

"What do you mean?"

"What I said, Marcus. Would you curse your best friend publicly, in front of everyone, while in your heart you praise him?"

"I would, to save my life," he retorted.

"Well, I won't, even if it costs me mine," she answered.

"He must be quite a friend, then."

"He is," she replied softly.

But Marcus would not give up. Once again he put both hands on her shoulders and looked at her steadily. He forced himself to use the most tender tone of voice that he could.

"Junia, dearest sister, think for a moment. Is this friend of yours worth more to you than your family, than your future husband, than your own life? Certainly no friend can be worth that much. No true friend would want you to suffer so."

Junia slipped from her brother's grasp and started to dance, very gracefully, to the other side of the room. It was a Corinthian dance that Marcia had taught her.

"Junia, what on earth are you doing?"

"I'm being grateful to you."

"Why?"

Suddenly Junia ran back to him and put her arms around him.

"Because you're so good, and because you defended me in public."

Marcus blushed and made a grimace.

"How did you find out about that?"

"Cynthia told me. News travels fast in the city, both good and bad. Marcus, thank you for defending me; I know you didn't have to do it. I am convinced that I have the best brother in all of Rome."

Marcus looked at her sadly.

"And I'm convinced that I have the best sister in the whole world, but I'm going to lose her."

VII.

The date for Junia's execution was finally set. All of Rome had been waiting for it, since it was clear that she would never offer wine and incense to the Emperor's image. What amazed most of the common people was that Gaius was still named consul, and his family continued to be one of the most honored in the city. Some people maintained that

Junia herself had appealed to the Emperor, making him see that her own belief in no way compromised her parents or her brother. Others felt that the Emperor simply realized that Gaius was too good a choice to lose, and that he would make an excellent consul despite his daughter's perverse religion.

Though Gaius was duly named consul, he had to do something beforehand that deeply repulsed him. He was forced to sign a statement formally disowning his daughter. He asked if he could simply denounce her religion, but it was not enough; the law was clear. One week afterward Junia was sentenced to die by beheading in the amphitheatre—a decision that Gaius struggled to negate with all his influence but could not. By that time the force of public opinion had become so strong that probably even the Emperor could not have saved her.

Two days before her execution date, Junia was transferred from the consul's mansion to a private house near the Vaticanus fields, where she was placed under guard. She was given good quarters, since she was a consul's daughter, but she was not allowed any visitors except for her personal maid and members of her family. She asked Marcus and Aurelia to tell her father that she understood why he had to disown her and that she had no bitterness toward him. Rather, she would pray for him and for the Emperor. Marcus and Aurelia could only nod sadly and helplessly; they could not understand her at all and thought that all of her suffering was foolishness. Her father never came to visit her.

After midnight of the first day she was left alone and spent a long time on her knees, looking at a small cross that she had fashioned from tying two twigs together. "Jesus, I love you," she whispered as she kissed it. "Help me to be strong for you."

This had helped her greatly. For days before the execution date was set, she had been torn by many doubts and fears. With the constant pressure from her family, especially her father, she began to wonder if she was doing the right thing. At one point she had even thought of running away. But each time she had prayed to Christ, the Good Shepherd, and had kissed the simple wood cross that she had made. She could feel him holding her firmly in his arms and Marcia smiling and praying for her.

At last she had gotten to the point that she felt no anxiety about what was going to happen to her. On the contrary, she felt very happy that God had answered her prayers—nothing adverse had happened to her family on account of her. She had prayed intensely for that. Gaius had been appointed consul, and her family continued in its high position in Rome.

She tried to sleep afterward but then she laughed to herself. How silly it was to try to sleep when one was going to lose one's head tomorrow! Early in the morning she rose and began to read a scroll that she had brought with her. It was a text that she had carefully copied from one of Paul's letters to the Romans, written almost eighty years earlier. She liked it especially since it had a word from Jesus' own language, Aramaic. With a prayer she read it again, this time more slowly and with great attention:

"For whoever are led by the Spirit of God, they are the children of God. Now you have not received a spirit of bondage so as to be again in fear, but you have received a spirit of adoption as sons, by virtue of which we cry 'Abba, Father.'"

She stopped for a moment and thought of her father. She owed so much to him, almost all that was humanly good in her, she reflected. But he could not give her the greatest gift. She prayed for him tenderly and asked that one day he too might become a Christian. Then she continued to read:

"The Spirit himself gives testimony to our spirit that we are children of God. But if we are children, we are heirs also:

heirs indeed of God and joint heirs with Christ, provided, however, we suffer with him that we may also be glorified with him."

For a moment she thought of Marcia and her father, Diodorus. How lucky Marcia was to have her father with her in heaven. They had suffered together with Christ. If God so willed, very soon she would be joining them.

GLORY

It was a clear Spring day in Rome. The amphitheatre owners could not have been happier, being sure now that huge crowds would attend the games, and witness the execution. It seemed that everyone in the city was anxious to get a glimpse of the newly condemned Christian: apart from being the daughter of a consul, she was considered to be one of the most beautiful young women in Rome.

The road from Junia's place of custody was lined with people, with an unusual mixture of plebeians and patricians, freedmen and slaves. All were interested in the spectacle, as so many had been in the execution of Ignatius years before, during Trajan's reign. There were excited comments along with many crude jokes. "Will they treat her like they did the last one . . . that Corinthian girl?" "Nah," someone answered quickly, "she's royalty almost. Just beheading for her."

Many of them expected to see an hysterical girl writhing and shouting and cursing Caesar. It was not that way. As the large chariot used for conveying prisoners wound through the streets of the city, Junia stood erect, with her dark hair waving in the breeze. She was clothed in a simple white tunic at her request, and her face looked totally calm. She even seemed to be smiling as she rode past them, as if she were secretly pleased by something.

Discalus had closed his fish store for the occasion. Though he did not plan to go to the games, he wanted to see the condemned Christian, at least once; he brought his small son so that he too could get a glimpse of the notorious lady. As the chariot drew closer, there were shouts of "Christian! Traitor!" "Dishonor to your father!" "You deserve worse than this, you whore. . . ." Many people had fists in the air. Discalus lifted his boy to his shoulders so that he could see her.

After the chariot had passed by, Discalus lowered his son to the ground. "What did you see?" he asked him. His son looked up at him excitedly. "A very pretty lady dressed in white. She smiled at me, Father, and waved. She's brave." Discalus, clearly disappointed at his son's reaction, scowled and struck him on the side of the head. "Don't be foolish. Didn't I tell you that she was a Christian?" "And can't Christians be brave?" asked a hoarse voice from a man standing immediately beside them. He said it as though he had been debating something long and hard within him. Though he was a well-built athletic looking young man, there were tears in his eyes and he seemed to be trembling. Discalus thought that he recognized the face; it was someone that he had once seen marching in the Praetorian Guard.

Junia's lips moved steadily as the chariot advanced through the crowded streets. She was thanking the Savior for the privilege of sharing his cross at that moment, including the insults. Scintilla had told her that the crowds had also insulted *him* very badly when he had to carry the cross through the streets of Jerusalem. "What's more," Junia thought to herself with a bit of humor, "I am lucky enough to have a chariot; he had nothing."

Junia could recognize some familiar faces in the crowds. She couldn't see Scintilla or Justus's family, but she knew they were among the people, and in her heart she could feel them praying for her. At one point she saw her father's assistant Bombolinus in one of the front rows—and nodded to him with a smile. Bombo looked away quickly, his face very red. "Do you know her?" someone asked who was standing close by. "No!" Bombolinus grumbled back, as he began to elbow his way through the people. "But wait, don't you work for Gaius?" "No," he shouted back, "I swear I've never seen her before."

At one turn, as the chariot approached the amphitheatre entrance, Junia's heart skipped a beat. About thirty feet ahead, to her left, she could see Livia and her mother. They were silent compared to the rest of the shouting crowds; they seemed almost sad to her. "Father, forgive them," she prayed silently. She was grateful for the opportunity to imitate Christ once again, who had also prayed for his enemies. As the chariot passed by, she looked at them briefly, then turned her head.

Once in the amphitheatre, Junia was escorted to a special chamber within the theatre itself. There would be about a three-hour wait until her execution . . . to give time for the crowds to arrive and for the first event, which was a fight between two gladiators and a lion from Numidia. She could hear the shouts from the stands, mixed with booing and applause. Cynthia was with her, by special permission. She was trembling; the entire thing was so horrible for her that she could not sit still.

Junia tried to soothe her. "Don't cry, Cynthia. Just consider me another gladiator."

Cynthia shook her head slowly and looked to the ground. "Miss, I don't know how you can joke in a moment like this."

"Do you know what Scintilla told me about Marcia when she died?"

"No, what did she tell you?"

"When they did that brutal thing to her, she was singing. Imagine that, Cynthia; she was singing! Because she knew that she was going straight to the almighty and good One. They're going to be much more merciful with me, it seems. A stroke of the axe, and it is finished. If Marcia could sing, the least I can do is smile."

But Cynthia continued to tremble; she was beginning to cry and sob loudly. Junia ran to her and embraced her.

"Don't cry, dear friend. I'm going to a place of great happiness, to be with the Good Shepherd and his mother, forever. You should be happy for me. . . ."

At that she paused and looked at her servant intently. She couldn't hide the expectation in her voice when she said, "Have you come to believe in Jesus, Cynthia?"

Cynthia looked away from her mistress. Her voice was wavering.

"You've told me so many things, Junia. And I have thought about them a lot, but I still don't know. I can't decide. It seems so hard to be a Christian; and you have to give up so much."

"I'll pray for you more," the aristocratic Roman girl answered back cheerfully. "I'm sure," she added with a chuckle, "that you wouldn't want to repeat my story, if you were to become a Christian."

Cynthia laughed for the first time since she had come to join her mistress. But she could not speak. All she knew was that someone wonderful was about to leave her life, someone who had sincerely cared about her and her father. She looked at Junia's face; it was radiant, more beautiful than she could remember before.

Without warning the cell door was flung open. A burly prison guard entered and barked out gruffly: "Come on, in there. Let's go!"

"Right away, sir," Junia answered immediately. "We can't keep the people waiting, can we?"

Cynthia was on her knees, crying. Junia stooped over her and cupped her servant's face between her hands. "I'm going now, my dear friend, and I shall pray for you. Take this please, and read it after they've beheaded me. It has given me courage throughout the entire ordeal. I hope it will help you, too. I love you dearly."

After giving Cynthia a papyrus roll that had been carefully resealed, Junia kissed her friend and very nimbly, almost like an athlete, she skipped to the door where the guard waited for her.

"Now I shall really dance, Cynthia . . . forever!" the comely girl shouted, and disappeared from her sight.

Cynthia could hear the crowds roaring as Junia was led to the block in the middle of the amphitheatre. "Down with the Christians!" they were chanting. Close to the cell door she could hear one man shouting: "Serves her right." Cynthia covered her ears for a moment; her sight was blurred with tears. She couldn't even distinguish the sunlight flowing in generously between the cell bars. All of a sudden the crowds stopped shouting: there was an immense hush in the entire stadium. Cynthia knew that Junia was about to be killed. Instinctively she clutched the papyrus scroll very close to herself. Within a few seconds the shouting began again, this time mixed with obscenities.

Cynthia remained kneeling on the stone floor; she did not know for how long. At last she was able to focus her vision and saw the sunlight once again, entering the small cell cheerfully, as if nothing had happened, and the clear blue sky above Rome. Slowly, very deliberately she unrolled what Junia had entrusted to her. It was a letter . . . the same letter that Marcia had written to Junia, just twelve months before.

Finis.